FRAGILE

FRAGILE

CHRIS KATSAROPOULOS

To my friend Jack,
Best wishes
Chris
3/12/10

LUMINIS BOOKS

LUMINIS BOOKS
Published by Luminis Books
13245 Blacktern Way, Carmel, Indiana, 46033, U.S.A.
Copyright © Chris Katsaropoulos, 2009

Cover design and composition for *Fragile* by Joanne Riske.

ISBN-10: 1-935462-27-X

ISBN-13: 978-1-935462-27-9

Printed in the United States of America

10 9 8 7 6 5 4 3 2 1

On the earth the broken arcs; in the heaven a perfect round.

Robert Browning

Or ever the silver cord be loosed, or the golden bowl be broken, or the pitcher be broken at the fountain, or the wheel broken at the cistern. Then shall the dust return to the earth as it was: and the spirit shall return unto God who gave it.

Ecclesiastes, 12:6 – 12:7

ℭ

INSTEAD OF SKIPPING out to lunch for half an hour, Holly has to take a walk-in who wants a full cut and color. Holly tries to slip past the front desk and down the stairs, but the insolent girl working the desk calls her over with a smirk and points to the old woman trying to situate herself in one of the sleek, cone-shaped plastic chairs in the waiting area.

"I would've given her to Trent," the girl whispers slyly, "but he has a two o'clock coming." Then she adds what amounts to a warning. "She wants a special."

Holly nods and wonders what she's in for this time. Ever since she started running around with Rick Oester, the bartender at the Midtown Grill, Holly's business has taken a nosedive. She leaves the kids with her mother and stays out late, drinking too much, smoking too much, waiting for Rick to close. Then, when it's 2 a.m., maybe 3, they go out—or, more often, they end up at his place. The next morning, she feels like death warmed over, and the customers notice. She's been late to her morning appointments and missed a few altogether. Now she has big one-hour, two-hour gaps in her book, and this is what she gets: Whatever leftovers wander in off the street.

1

"How are *you?*" Holly says, trying to perk up her voice and hide the disappointment in her face. She extends her hand to the old woman, who has found herself trapped by the peculiar ergonomics of the tipped-up cone chair, more an offer of assistance than a greeting. The woman places her hand into Holly's and latches on with a surprisingly forceful grip. The appendage Holly holds in her hand has a curious parchment-like feel to it, as if a small sack of bones has suddenly sprung to life and grasped the first thing that passed by. Holly's initial reaction is to let go, but the old woman's hand clutches at her as she tries to pull away. The cool skin of the hand is thin and papery, the round knobs of the knuckles bulging white as the woman yanks on Holly's arm to hoist herself up.

"My foot fell asleep," she says, gasping from the effort of raising herself. "No circulation. These chairs send all the blood to your . . . " she gasps again audibly, as Holly gives her one last tug to get her on her feet, "to your backside."

"I guess they're not built for—" and then she stops short, trying to come up with a kinder way to say *old people.* The only thing she can think of that doesn't sound offensive is "senior citizens," but the words feel awkward and mean as they come out of her mouth. The woman glances at Holly and lets go of her hand. "I'm Holly, by the way. We're heading over here," she says, striding towards the row of hair-washing sinks lined up beneath the tall picture windows on the far side of the shop. High above their heads, huge, four-spoked ceiling fans slowly churn the air. The heels of Holly's beige pumps click with a solemn purpose on the hardwood floors, adding a staccato beat to the undulating whine of Trent's blow drier as he waves it over the head of his one-thirty. The fronds of the large potted plants quiver from the currents of air circulating around the shop. Holly points to an open basin and watches the woman carefully lower her head into it, resting the base of her skull against the dip where the neck goes.

Holly steps to the back of the basin, looking at the woman's tired upside down face from a great height. From this vantage point, the normal geometry of the face is inverted, giving Holly precisely what she wants—the true picture of what she has to work with, the hair separate from the nose, the mouth, the eyes; an entity unto itself. She makes a quick assessment before the wash: faded blond tinged by gray, a respectable cut with layers feathering back over the ears, collar length—maybe a bit too long for a woman this old. How old is she really? Holly wonders. It's not the kind of question she can ask directly, and that's the problem with picking up these strays off the street. With her regulars, she can work with a known quantity, rejoin the conversation in mid-beat from the previous appointment—"How are the kids? Oh, a new dog? What kind? How sweet." There's more effort with a walk-in, finding out what they like and don't like in their cut, making small talk about the weather. Long periods of silence such as this.

"So," Holly says, staring into the upside down eyes of the old woman, "what are we doing here today?"

"My name's Amelia," the old lady says. "I had trouble finding this place, upstairs and all. One of my dear friends said you could help."

A referral—it's been a while since she's had one of those. As she's been losing her stockpile of regulars, she's also been losing the people they recommend her to. She reaches down and touches the woman's hair lightly, getting a feel for it before she washes.

"Really?" Holly says. "What's your friend's name?"

"Dolores," the old woman says. "Dolores King."

Holly sifts through a list of names, faces, customers she has or once had, even friends of customers, and finds that the name means nothing to her. Then she realizes: Dolores King didn't refer Amelia to Holly. The girl at the desk said she would have given her to Trent.

"Dolores told me this place has the best beauticians in town." Holly nearly laughs to hear her use such an old-fashioned word. "About a year ago, the lady who used to do my hair—did it for more than twenty years—passed away. Since then, I've tried a lot of places, but no one can get it right. The color is off somehow, the length of the bangs is never right. Then I tell them it's wrong and they look at me like I'm some kind of crazy old coot."

Amelia glances up at Holly with a kind of stern defiance, as if to rebuke all the other haircutters who have given her poor cuts. Holly touches her hair again, gently lifting it away from the compartment of the sink and letting it fall strand by strand. She still has plenty to work with, not thinning like she sees in many women Amelia's age. Lots of hair, but very fine, like the angel hair in the hollow center of the ornament they used to cautiously place on the top bough of the Christmas tree when she was a child. The light catches each filament as they fall away from her hand: silver, white, gray, gold. No roots, not a trace of auburn or black. Clearly, there's been some coloring, but it's hard to tell how much.

"Oh, you're not crazy," Holly says. "You just want what you want."

"Can you help me? I'm looking for something . . . special. My fiftieth high school reunion is tomorrow night."

"And you want to look great. Let's wash up here, and you can tell me all about it."

Holly starts the water from the jet nozzle at the end of the hose and adjusts the temperature to warm the water. Then she soaks Amelia's hair, transforming it from a fine halo of golden gray into a limp solid mass that hangs from her head, dark and slick. She spurts a glob of fragrant shampoo into her palm and plies it onto Amelia's glimmering head, massaging the scalp, working her fingers into the hair. In all the years she's been cutting hair for a living, Holly has never tired of this part of the job. Weaving her fingers into the heavy, wet hair of her customer, she lowers her voice and murmurs a reassurance that everything will be okay, she will take care of her. She can feel the tension ease out of this woman as her eyes close and she slumps lower in the reclining black leather chair. Once again in this second-story shop high above ground, the inexorable force of gravity pulls Amelia's body towards the earth. Holly's fingertips press into the contours of Amelia's skull, massaging the scalp, exploring the interlocking bones of the crown. She works her way around to the sides of the head, probing the soft areas

5

around the temples. In the hidden pockets behind each ear, a knob of bone protrudes and there are paired clefts, indentations where the plastic earpieces of Amelia's glasses have worn their way into the soft bone over the decades, two groovelike canyons. Our bodies are surprisingly pliant, conforming themselves to the forces that mold us day by day, year after year. Holly's hand

wends its way across the top of my head, pressing hard, now doing something with the water, squirting another glob of shampoo or maybe conditioner. This time it smells like cocoanuts, like a tropical drink with chemicals from a perm someone else is getting mixed in, tingling at the top of my head and down my back. It hurts where this hard sink presses into my neck. If she doesn't stop soon, I will have to tell her, but it feels so good where she massages that I don't want it to be over. I'd come back to this woman again just to have her wash my hair this way, but I doubt if she can cut it as well as Claire used to. No one else has been able to, why should she? Dolores says this shop is the best, so maybe this Holly will be as good as Claire was, but will you ever see me Tris? We could meet at the show, at the five o'clock show like we used to, or I could see you at the lunch counter at Haag's and have a soda, you know there's no point in avoiding me any longer. We could be together again, the way it was before. We could see each other every day, but you have to come now.

They say they're going to tear the Lyceum down, Tris. It's not a big hotel and theater anymore, now a boarding house for old people like us. They say they're going to knock it down with

a big wrecking ball, crumbling to a pile of dust, the whole wonderful thing falling into itself, all the beautiful carpets and the
walls inside, the pastel walls cracking into a pile of dust and
rubble. They're going to knock it all down and then the phone
is ringing, playing a tune. Her hands went away, digging in her
pocket. "Hang on a sec," the phone is playing a tune.

The fan twirls up by the ceiling, and it's cold in here with my
hair wet. The frond of the potted plant waves at me, "No Mom,
I can't tell him to forget it . . . That's fine, if you insist on
screwing up my life again, you've done it so many times before.
Well, how can I ever repay you for that?. . . No, you go ahead.
I'll find someone else to watch them." She clicks the phone
shut and twirls around behind me, her face high up, her chin,
and the dark holes of her nose release a heavy sigh. She stares
ahead at the empty space above me not looking down, not doing anything, filled with rage. "What's the matter?"

she   says,

tilting her head back and peering up at Holly from the dark confines of the sink. Holly doesn't want this old woman to be here,
doesn't want her prying into her problems, her battles with her
mother. For an instant, the old woman in the sink has *become* her
mother, the head that stares up at her is the same as the fearful,
reprimanding head of her mother, a sink full of shoulds and
do's and don'ts calling up to her from somewhere in the depths
of her soul, telling her what she must do and berating her when
she doesn't obey the commands. Though the voice that floats
up to her is meant to be helpful, it fills her with dread, eats away
at the thin membrane that protects the innermost part of her

7

from the outside. Then, a wheel in her head turns a notch, and she knows she must answer the question.

"Nothing really," Holly says. "Babysitter problem." She grabs a fistful of the woman's hair and squeezes, ringing the water out.

"You sound upset." The whites of the old woman's eyes rotate further back into their sockets. Trying to get a better look at Holly. "Is there any way I can help?"

You could shut up and go away, Holly thinks. She squeezes the hair tighter and imagines herself starting to pull, yanking the head down. If you pulled on the wet rope of hair hard enough, you could easily snap a person's neck against the fulcrum created by the smooth lip of the sink. The skin on Amelia's face looks like parchment, like the high-resolution color x-ray pictures of a mummy she saw in a news magazine recently, layers of papery parchment the color of a grocery sack bronzed with great age. The reedy lips move almost imperceptibly, the tongue still remarkably pink behind yellowed teeth and flaring gums, blowing puffs of stale breath, forming another set of words.

"If you need a babysitter," the old woman says, "perhaps I can help you. You have kids that need watching, and I've got nothing but time on my hands."

The words are so incongruous with the images flitting through Holly's head that it takes a moment for Holly to process what she's saying. She has never left her two girls with anyone but her mother. And as vexing as her mother can be, Holly feels confident that nothing bad will happen to the girls at her mother's house. Plus, leaving them there frees her to stay out all night if she wants. Her implacable need for Rick injects itself into her thinking, races through the air above their heads like the swift shadow of a jet plane on its way to the point where it will meet with the jet itself on the runway when the plane touches down.

"Well," Holly says, calculating, getting down to business, "where do you live? I mean, I usually drop my girls off at my Mom's house—instead of having someone come by." The force of habit, the power of her need, frames her thinking: She wants to leave the girls at someone else's house, as she normally does. In the instant before Amelia answers, she tries to picture where someone like Amelia would live, and the results are not good. She imagines linoleum floors and empty tins of cat food stacked on the kitchen counter. Flock wallpaper and mildewy shag carpet, tinged with the smell of mothballs. A trailer park or an old farmhouse in a cornfield outside of town.

"I'm on the number 8 bus line. East Washington. I take the 8 downtown, and the 15 over here." Then Amelia adds, in a voice lacking any hint of embarrassment. "I don't drive, you see."

Amelia's lips form themselves into a broad, unassuming smile, a pressed shallow arc that reminds Holly of pictures she has seen of FDR's wife smiling in spite of hard times. Holly knows she must choose soon or the offer will be withdrawn, an idea whose sheer absurdity is revealed by gradual exposure to the light of day. The faces of her two girls loom before her, images that have been stylized in her mind's eye from dozens of photographs she has hanging on the walls of her home and mounted in art frames on the table behind this sink in the salon: Jenny and Zoe standing next to a snowman they helped her build, their faces beaming with joy; their first family portrait together, the one with their father still in it; a Polaroid of Jenny from her fourth birthday party, the father no longer there, chocolate icing smeared across her chubby cheeks. And then the shadow of Rick's need darting past, her own need racing to meet it. Holly says

"What time can you take them?" as if they are a burden to be unloaded. She twists my hair again to wring the excess water from it. Don't worry. Though I haven't even seen them, they are just as precious to me. I have taken care of children before, and Tris and I were children once together. We played in the yard behind the house in Elmer's garden, we ran behind the big swing, wrestled in the hammock.

"Whenever you need to bring them by. I can give them dinner, if you want." We ran behind the swing and wrestled in the hammock. Tris had his arm around me and Elmer came by, Tris called out and rolled over, his weight tipped the hammock hanging between the two ends of the pole, he tipped it and fell out. She stares down at me with her eyes dazzled, glazed over by her wanting. It's okay, I want to say to her, it's okay for you to want a man. I wanted someone too. I wanted him, but he tipped and fell out. He fell and chipped his tooth, blood spilling across the grass. He fell and I wanted him even more, he fell and he

slips the plastic card into the slot, the green light blinks above it, the door yields with a satisfying click, and he is in. The maids have turned the air conditioning down too low, as usual—all these air conditioned spaces he inhabits, airports, rental car buses, hotels, restaurants, convention centers, are chilled to a temperature that's uncomfortable without a sweater, a sports coat, or a long-sleeved shirt, as if the wonder of air conditioning is not self evident without cooling the room to sixty-five degrees. He tosses the overnight bag on the bed and tests it, dropping his weight onto the side edge and bouncing up and down a couple of times—not too bad, firm. Plenty of pillows and several different sizes. He will use some for sleeping on his back, other larger ones for sleeping on his side, propping his head up at just the right angle to avoid getting a stiff neck.

In his years of travel for work he has become a connoisseur of hotel rooms, and though he is not a snob about it, he understands there are certain things that will make the brief segment of his life he is wasting in this rented space more tolerable. He always requests a king instead of two queens, because it means the large faux mahogany or cherry cabinet that holds the television will more likely be situated directly in front of the bed for optimal viewing—again, he avoids the stiff neck because he won't have to turn his head at an awkward angle to see the screen. He always requests non-smoking. There is an iron and ironing board. Wireless internet has become a must as well, though he notes that minibars have become much less frequent denizens of these tight, temporary compartments where he spends a good portion of his life. Too much pilferage? The only reason he can imagine for them to eliminate the profit center that provides the $6.00 cans of beer and $4.00 packages of candy he used to enjoy. The obligatory small couch or chair fronted by a coffee table. The work desk and lamp, all furnishings in a comforting traditional style. The print of ducks on the wing or a bland, non-threatening landscape hanging on the otherwise blank walls.

He avoids the trendy, modern boutique hotels because they usually get something wrong in their efforts to be funky and bizarre. He drags the heavy curtains aside and opens the shades, letting the late afternoon sunlight filter in through the dust. A view of a parking lot and a city he will not even bother to explore. To him it is just another airport, another meeting. It could be Denver or Des Moines or Detroit just the same. Many years ago, in the first decade he traveled, he used to try to walk the cities he visited, to avoid being completely sedentary and to get to know the place. Now the thought of going beyond the constricted tube of airport/hotel/conference center/office space is repugnant to him. The more he sleeps and watches television, the sooner the trip will be over.

He pulls a wrinkled dress shirt out of the overnight bag and hangs it in the closet tucked behind the wall that partitions the vanity from the rest of the room and, as he sees himself doing these things, he catches himself thinking about himself in the third person again, as if he is a kind of benign, observant, godlike being or one of those tiny security cameras mounted in a corner of the room tracking the actions of this person who has entered and disturbed the muffled silence of the place—not a person so much as a sequence of states and events that lead smoothly from one to another to another until the ultimate and final event has occurred. In a swift instant his awareness has skipped outside itself and he has lost all sense of being a single, unique person—Mr. Holloway was the name they addressed him by at the front desk—and instead he sees himself as merely an aperture for experiencing the sensations of this world for a brief time, a tiny hole that has opened in the fabric of time and space to capture bits of light and vibration, converting electro-magnetic waves into images and sounds. Why me? Why this person, here, in this room: Tristan Holloway? He feels himself rising to a great height, outside himself, the world melting away beneath him. He has left behind whatever it was that comprised his self, and the sensation is one of dizzying freedom— everything that went into making this person, Tristan Holloway, is momentarily no longer there. In its place, a vast emptiness, the aperture expanding to encompass everything outside that narrow tube that was him.

The odd sensation is gone in a second.

Tristan Holloway finds himself standing in front of the closet again, staring at his blue dress shirt hanging on the hanger where he hung it a moment ago. He takes a deep breath and feels the hole he fell up through tightening around himself again. The aperture closes to a tight little point.

He walks to the bed and picks up another dress shirt, hangs it in the closet. Then, instead of finishing unpacking, he slips off his shoes and lies down on the

bed where Tris and I used to lie down when they made us take naps in the afternoon. We were all up here, Louise and Elmer, me and Tris, and they made us take naps, but we never slept, running around hiding and making noise, talking until one of them came up to quiet us. I could let the girls sleep here in this bed or maybe in Karl's room, the single room in back, if they have to stay all night. She wants them to stay all night, and everything's ready, they can stay all night and all the next day if she wants. I have taken care of children before, and Tris and I were children once together. He saw me, then I touched him. Now the bell is ringing, it's her ringing twice, she must be in a hurry.

"Hang on a sec!" The stairs are still narrow and steep. At the landing you can go either way, towards the front or the back, but on Elmer's side you can only go one way through the living room and she's ringing again. "Hold on!" She's not patient, young and wanting her man. The children are standing behind her, their faces hiding and cut into slats by the venetian blinds, jiggle the lock and the door opens with a catch. She steps through

      the doorway and into the dank living room, not what she would consider impoverished but slightly musty somehow, the furniture must be fifty years old most of it, antiques in all likelihood. Maybe some of it is worth something, if the old lady ever had the inclination to sell. A flattened recliner floats in the middle of the room aimed at the television, flanked by a teetering oval end table draped by a lace doily stained with yellow arcs, empty cans of diet soda, and a half-eaten bag of corn chips. Holly envisions the hours the old lady must spend slouched in the tan nappy chair soaking up afternoon soap operas, her body sinking into the plush overstuffed fabric, slowly becoming one with it—as soft and pliable as it is. But Amelia it seems has dressed up for this occasion. Her hair is of course looking much better since this afternoon, trimmed and a better fit for her head, a long head with cheeks that have become jowly over the years, loose flesh hanging and drooping a bit as you would expect, the cheeks spotted with bright patches of rouge Amelia has applied. Her eyebrows have been tended to carefully, plucked and primed to a fine cambering line over each glimmering eye. She has on what Holly would consider to be nothing less than a pant suit constructed from acres of pastel blue synthetic fabric, a relic from the seventies or early eighties—what a woman from that prehistoric age would wear for a day at the office, clearly dragged out of the closet as a means of putting on her best for Holly and the girls.

Holly extends her hand tentatively, and for the second time this day Amelia takes it. They don't shake in the direct one-to-one grasp of two businessmen. Instead, it is more a brief holding of hands, the way women do. The grip from Amelia is taut, more full of feeling for her, but the bones are still there, still swimming it seems beneath the thin mottled skin she felt before, blue veins surging in gnarled meandering channels across the top of the hand. Holly lets go first, but she tries to convey through her touch a multiplicity of meanings: how much this help means to her, how grateful she is and also how hard it is to leave her girls here.

"Come inside girls," Amelia says, reaching to the bureau that crouches along the wall by the door. "I have a treat for each of you."

Startled and enticed by the prospect of what the old lady hides in her hands, Jenny and Zoe move towards her with furtive shy steps, their heads downturned but peering at the two arms hiding something behind her broad backside.

"Pick one," she says, challenging. "Go ahead." Jenny, being the oldest, after a tick of hesitation, steps forward and points to Amelia's left arm. It comes out from behind her and the hand opens to reveal a pale blue ball the size of a large marble, speckled with pinpricks and swirls of white, a miniature model of an earth-like planet. Jenny stares at it, not quite knowing what to do.

"Now you. You must be Zoe. The youngest."

She nods her head almost imperceptibly and points to the other arm, as if she still has a choice in the matter. The right hand appears and releases another swirling blue marble, nearly identical to the first. Both girls are surprised by getting the same thing—they thought the act of choosing a hand meant there would be two different gifts. They look towards their mother as if to inquire whether this is all quite right. Holly smiles to reassure them.

"They're jawbreakers, special candy," Amelia says. "You don't eat them—they're too hard to chew. But if you suck on them for a long time, they change colors and taste different too."

Holly peeks beyond the exaggerated shoulders of Amelia's suit jacket towards the dining room.

"Is there a phone . . . I can use?"

Jenny has popped the blue ball into her mouth, her cheek bulging from the effort to contain and control it. She bites down once, testing, and her teeth crack against the unyielding rock in her mouth.

"Don't bite," Amelia says, heading for the dining room. "They'll break your teeth." She points at a beige desk phone complete with a cord and a rotary dial, almost as old as the furniture. Holly picks up the handset and begins to dial, plugging her finger in the notch for the first number and pulling it around to the dull tusk of metal that stops her. The dial tone hums and then is interrupted by a series of clicks that signifies the number going through.

It takes a while to dial this way, but it still works. Rick comes to the phone after one of the cooks tracks him down. Busy kitchen noise, people talking, pots and pans clattering in the background. His voice is strained.

"Yes," Holly says. "I think it'll be okay." She turns her back and faces away from Amelia, who has drifted towards the living room and is talking to the girls. "A nice old lady." Holly listens out of her other ear to catch what Amelia and the girls are saying. "The neighborhood? Not so great. There are Mexicans next door." But she tells him what he wants to hear. "No—it's okay. Really. I'll be there soon," knowing full well that he doesn't get off until midnight, if then.

Holly looks around the dining room, her mind's eye scanning it as she listens to Rick complain about work, neither one of these inputs fully registering. A table and four chairs. Old as the furniture in the front room. Rick saying the bastard was

17

supposed to come in so I don't have to close. A hulking break-front that looks handmade—a real antique maybe—with a display of silver-framed photographs on the lower shelves. And on top of the breakfront a fine porcelain vase, more of a pitcher really, now that she looks, a vessel meant for carrying liquids, the only lovely thing she's seen in this house, the modulation of its curves evoking nothing more than the dip of a woman's waist as the line goes dead—he's

gone to school, a bright young man they all said, you'll be a famous architect Tris, designing grand buildings like the Lyceum Theater. The girls are playing with the animal cards, the game I gave them, Flinch or Pit. The oldest lays a card down and the other puts down three, they don't even know how to play. We could've had girls like this, two lovely girls, I would have given you children like when we played house together. I was always the mother and you were the father and Elmer was the child and Louise would never play, off doing something else, too grown up for us. She was always better, and we always thought she would tell

me   your phone number so I can have it, just in case." In case, Holly thinks. In case something happens to the girls. Amelia writes the number with a blue pencil that says GRAIN DEALERS MU-TUAL ASSURANCE along one side of it, in tiny white block letters. And just as Holly is gathering the nerve to take her leave, one last look at the girls before saying goodbye, she's startled by a black moth that flutters into her frame of vision and brushes against her face. She jerks her head back, flinching, as her hand comes up involuntarily trying to sweep it away. "Jesus!" she says, swiping at it again, and the moth dances away, fluttering towards the ceiling, dancing around the crenellated light fixture that holds the two bare bulbs in place.

"Must have come in with you and the girls," Amelia says. "Here, before you go. Let me show you my garden."

Holly tries to gather herself after her brush with the black moth, which flutters and dips its way around the light. Her heart is still racing from being startled.

"Oh," she says, not knowing what to say. She doesn't really want to see any garden. Rick is waiting for her, her need for him bearing down on them, pressing out across the miles. "Sure. I bet it's a wonderful garden."

"It is," Amelia says, holding out her hand for the girls to follow. "It certainly is."

The lots in this workingman's slum are long and narrow like the houses they contain. The sidewalks from the back doors at each side of the double angle towards each other, forming a Y, the resulting single sidewalk heading towards the garage and alley at the far end of the yard. A towering oak tree shades the Mexicans' portion of the yard, its shadow cutting across from Amelia's side where a round bed of flowers nestles underneath the thick trunk. The girls take off towards the bird bath, and before Holly can stop them start splashing their hands in the water held by the shallow plaster dish.

"It's okay," Amelia says. "I change it every day."

There's a bird feeder on a metal pole nearby and a long narrow flower bed flanking the fence on the Mexicans' side, forming a river of color to separate Amelia's domain from the ragged and trash-strewn lot of the house next door. The August evening is beginning to settle in, the insistent dry chirring of the cicadas swells to a crescendo, gathering itself then quickly dying away, the leaves of the trees swaying in the first cool breeze that signals a hint of autumn coming. Holly watches as a starling lands on the lip of the birdbath, peers at its reflection in the water for a moment, then, with a casual flip of its wings, darts away.

"The neighbors are good people, the Salgados. They let me keep my beds after Elmer passed away." She must mean the Mexicans in the other half of the double. Amelia is walking towards the long phalanx of flowers along the far side of the yard, pointing to one of the splotches of color there. "My asters," she says. "Just starting to come in. Early this year. Black-eyed Susans and phlox. Cone flowers and snap dragons. Lord, how I love my snap dragons."

The girls have run to a bench-like swing that hangs from an inverted U-shaped iron pole towards the rear of the yard. Together they're sitting in the swing and laughing, their legs pumping in rhythm at the back of the arc, kicking against the air to make the bench go higher with each tinkling chink of the loose end of the chain as it swings them up into the sky. Holly's mind freezes them in a slow-motion vision captured at the top of arc, a holographic moment captured and bound up into the giant ball of emotion that rests within her, the girls' laughter and the pink and white and purple of the flowers swirled together into the knowledge that they will be safe here. Amelia will keep them safe.

"I don't know anything about gardening," Holly confesses. "Never had time for it." She gazes at the garden once more, her eyes trying to associate the names of the various flowers Amelia has just listed with the dazzling shapes and hues she sees before her. "Which ones are the snap

dragons?" she says, knowing full well which ones. She must know in her head even though her mind won't tell her, she's just talking to fill the air with words. Her mind is somewhere else, but her head already must know that the ones with the delicate curved lips reaching out over the bright tongues inside are the snaps. They were always our favorites, and Elmer's favorites too. He gave them a special place near the back porch so he could see them from the kitchen window, so they were the first thing you saw when you stepped towards the garden. Still the first thing, because I kept it all the same for you, Tris. It's all still here just as you would remember. You'd never know a day had passed since we rode in the swingset, we kicked our legs high, just the way these girls are doing. We went higher, higher, just like these girls, and we would swing

his legs off the bed after an hour and a half of watching the television sports recap and two consecutive re-runs of a sitcom. He hadn't intended to lie in bed so long, but he wanted to check the pennant races and then a good episode came on when he was flipping through the channels. On the desk at the far end of the room, his cell phone plays a tune that he downloaded only yesterday, a synthesized classical melody that sounds familiar to him but whose name he cannot remember, or, most likely, he never even knew. He checks the number before answering and sees that it is one of his customers, probably trying to reach him to ask about a problem they're having with the product he sold them. The digital readout on the phone says it's past 6:30—past 8:30 on the east coast—after hours as far as he's concerned, so he presses the IGNORE button and lets it roll to voice mail.

He sits for a moment at the chair by the desk and picks up one of his loafers, about to slip it on, but he decides that it's too early to go down for dinner. Within the gentle hush of the air conditioning, between the worn pile of the tan Dacron carpeting and the granulated white moonscape of the acoustic ceiling tiles, there is nothing left inside the frigid crypt-like space of this room but him and his failed ambitions. A thought invades the smooth emptiness the television has forged within his skull: *You will never make a difference.*

He will never fulfill his childhood ambitions. All those things he dreamed he would do are gone; they have been worn away by years of doing what he was told he should do, by listening to the voices that told him, one by one, over and over, to do the right thing, to tow the line and do what's expected of him.

He takes a deep breath of the chilled air and leans his head back, staring at the ceiling. His life floats there above him like a sinuous, gently twisting tape measure, the years ticked off from one to sixty-five across the tapered, faintly glowing surface of this object he has unwittingly fashioned. It seems to have an ebb and flow to it, as if it's being nudged along by a current in a stream, and he realizes that the rightmost end of the tape is narrowing to a blurred tip that must be the future: wavering, dim and indistinct, as opposed to the bright shining surface on the other end of the spectrum, where his hopes and dreams shone like the sun.

Then, from this image of despair, a vision of an expense account dinner appears, enticing him with the prospect of a beer and a steak at the hotel restaurant. This is what his life has been reduced to now: the momentary pleasures of eating, sleeping, and ingesting pre-packaged mass entertainment. Go ahead, a voice inside him says, you deserve it. You worked hard today, traveled all the way from Spokane to wherever it is you are now. The line at the airport check-in counter was long, the line at the security checkpoint even longer. They made him take out his laptop and take off his shoes. Even subjected him to the indignities of the probing metal wand and the pat-down search after his loose change triggered the x-ray alarm. The customer he met with this morning was unconvinced—no, the model 2006ZX server doesn't have the capacity we need to manage the entire food processing plant we're bringing on line in six months, and the new model 2007YZ is at least fifty thousand over the competitor's comparable. They wouldn't listen to reason, didn't try to work with him as he showed them how they could make it work with a simple upgrade to the 2006ZX. He left them the specs, promised a call back tomorrow, checked the box off his to-do list, and dropped the rental car at the airport.

But some yearning remnant of that glowing bright end of the tape measure, some indistinct notion of his own immortality hidden away in a compartment deep within him makes him open his briefcase and pull out the pad of drawing paper and a mechanical pencil he bought last week at the art supply house near the university campus in the city where he lives. The blank sheet of paper feels rough in his hands as he slowly, carefully tears it from the pad. He places it on the desk and sets the pad aside, the empty white sheet staring up at him, challenging him to make the first move.

It has been at least ten years since he last attempted to draw. He reads blueprints for his job on occasion, when he's looking at plans for a plant or office park where a server he has sold is going to be installed, but they are highly technical schematics that show the details of the network cabling for large industrial factories, huge boxes of steel and pre-fab concrete slabs where grape jelly or precision electronic circuit boards or jet aircraft engines will be manufactured. He knows how to read these schematics, but the pinpoint of light that shines within him, a remnant of his earliest ideas about himself, still seeks something beyond this transactional application of his talent. The first mark on the page is the most difficult, the act of prime commitment that will introduce a definite direction to the work. Yet the bulk of the form he imagines has set itself before him, hovers in the near foreground, somewhere between his brow and the lamp on the desk, and takes him, by the pure act of willful envisioning, outside himself, outside the deep regrets and fears that have haunted him. The form establishes itself as two smoothly curving arcs, and that is the essential problem of perspective that must resolve itself in his mind before pencil can be put to paper: the building occupies one quadrant of the circle that is the central plaza of the small Midwestern city where he was born. He must see it from a particular vantage point and then translate that view into a certain shallowness of arc that is less than the degree you would see if the building were viewed from directly above or directly in front.

A plinking of raindrops on the windows behind the drawn shades gives him a rhythm to work to, gathers force and becomes a solid undercurrent of rushing water. Yes, he thinks, remembering. The viewpoint should be from the steps that lead down from the monument that occupies the center of the circular plaza. That is where the viewer would stand: not at the top of the steps where the tall plinth of the monument rises, but midway down so the perspective can take in the entire building, the full ninety degrees of arc, from Kendall Street all the way around to Jefferson, each end of it surmounted by a fantastic and elaborate cupola.

He closes his eyes and lets himself see it. Hovering before him in the darkness, a shallow arc, the essence of the form. His eyes open and he places pencil to paper. With one effortless sweep of his forearm he traces the line across the virginal page, lightly delineating the pure and uncorrupted loveliness of it. In an instant the line is finished, the page is cleaved in two. He has done it.

He stands and walks to the window. He tugs the heavy curtains aside and stares through beads of water at the lights of the cars inching their way along the street below, the headlights

coming

at us, careful girls, hold my hand before we cross the street. Wait now, wait until this car goes by."

The cars parked along here make it hard to see. Where do so many cars come from? They should park in the garages by the alley, but they're lazy and don't want to pull all the way around back. The tinkling of the bell the vegetable man rings, he rolls his truck down the street the opposite way. It must be Friday, a broad twinkling of the bell calling us to the truck, gears grinding down to slow and pull up at the curb.

"Hold onto my hands girls, while we cross. We look both ways."

"Evening Amelia."

"Hello Tassie, how have you been keeping?" Out here in her bathrobe and a pair of beat up sneakers; I must look like I just came from church or a funeral. Flecks of sunlight striking her black hair, she dyes it darker than coal.

"Who you got there?"

"This is Jenny, and this one's Zoe. Babysitting for a good friend of mine."

The Mexicans are out and the blacks too, all of them ambling out. If we go a little faster we can get there before it's a line. Five years ago, there wasn't a single Mexican on the block. Fifteen years ago not a single black, but things must change, always things must change. Now look, it says *Fruteria Los Com-*

padres on the truck. The vegetable man rings the broad bell twinkling, parks it and hops around to the back.

"Buenas noches, mi amigos y amigas. Vienes comprar mi excelentes productos del campo. Manzanas, tomates, melónes a la venta."

The words roll off his tongue like a song.

"What are you buying tonight, Amelia?"

Tassie cut in front, she had to get there first. The littlest one holds on tighter. All these strangers and the smells, green beans with a crisp dry smell of the dirt in the fields, and the peaches too ripe it seems. The full round smell of ripe peaches, they waited too long on those. Now the other man comes to help, Miguel is his name. I cannot speak a word, but he smiles and pointing there, there, he knows. A handful of beans in the metal scale hanging from the back of the truck, he nods and puts another handful on the scale, slides them in the bag, then the oldest girl takes the melon, not too big to carry

his   portfolio

down to the lobby and look for the restaurant on the other side of the trickling slate-backed fountain, the Atrium Lounge or some name such as that, they did a nice job with the porterhouse the last time he was here.

Even though it's a hotel restaurant, the plump blond waitress gives him a squinty look when he tells her he wants a table for one, as if what he has asked for is an impossibility. She swivels her head around, scanning the half-empty room with its cherry paneling and wall sconces that each generate a surprisingly dim cone of light, then brings her eyes back to him, still trying to decide whether to show him to a seat.

"Do you have a reservation?"

"Do I need one?"

"We generally recommend it," she says, as if reading from a cue card, "especially after six."

A familiar and unwelcome sensation crowds its way into his head, coalescing into a lingering thought: *I don't belong here.* Even though he has inhabited this earth for sixty-five years and for most of the past forty has earned a salary that places him in the top ninety-five percent of wage-earners on the planet, the feeling that he doesn't really deserve to be here still haunts him. Ever since he can remember, a persistent sense of displacement has trailed him wherever he goes, as if he is mistakenly living someone else's life. As if he should be somewhere else, doing something else.

"There are open tables," he points out, his voice rising, defensively stating the obvious.

"I know, sir," the waitress says, "but we have a party of thirteen coming at seven, as well as several four-tops." She gives the word *sir* a special emphasis that manages to convey her annoyance with him.

"Well, okay then. I suppose there are other restaurants nearby." Defeated, he turns to take his leave, though he typically tries to stay inside the hotel as much as possible on these business trips, rarely venturing outside into the nameless cities he visits. He plans his next move, the elevator ride back to the room to get a sports coat and an umbrella, walking in the rain in search of a decent place to eat. The waitress consults a laminated map of the restaurant's tables, then reaches a decision.

With a deft slight twitch of her hand, she marks an X through one of the tables with a black magic marker.

"Here," she says, jerking her head towards the back of the room. "I can give you number three." She bolts in the direction of a large aquarium that's embedded into one of the wood-paneled walls. He thinks of the rain again and the prospect of the porterhouse he remembers from last time and follows her. The table she leads him to is off by itself, wedged into a space between the aquarium and the swinging double doors to the kitchen. She tosses one of the thick leather-bound menus onto the table in front of the chair that faces the kitchen doors, but he sits in the other chair instead, the one with a view of the murky aquarium.

"Soup of the day is seafood gumbo. My name is Maggie," she says, back on track with her pre-rehearsed script. "Leo will be your server tonight."

He settles into his chair and watches Maggie waddle away, anticipating the sharp bitterness of a cold beer. A waiter swoops around the corner and bangs his forearm into the metal door with such force that the door whipsaws three times on its hinges after he's disappeared into the kitchen. Soon, another waiter zips by, holding aloft a circular tray loaded with steaks and the humped, steaming back of a bright red lobster.

The jaunty classical tune starts chiming on Tris's cell phone. He quickly flips it open to stop the noise. The blinking message on the screen reveals the name and number of the caller who launched the snippet of symphony:

LAURA HOLLOWAY 415-555-9256

The brief message, a tiny electronic packet transmitted across hundreds of miles and laden with a wealth of conflicted meanings and emotions, scrolls across the screen and winks out of existence before returning again, number by number, on the left side. Tris hesitates for an instant, then presses IGNORE. Like magic, the music stops, the name goes away, at least for a while. Then, as if to demonstrate that he cannot shirk his responsibilities quite so easily, the phone chimes again. He makes a mental note to download a new ring tune—this one has proven to be quite annoying. He flips the phone open anticipating another call from Laura, an immediate response to his rebuke, but it's Hal Pope from Integrated Logistics, the customer he flicked away earlier by not answering the phone. It's past 9 p.m. on the east coast—this must really be trouble. Tris grits his teeth and presses TALK.

"Tris Holloway."

"Yes, Tris. I've been trying to reach you."

"Hal," he says with forced enthusiasm. "Kinda late out there."

"We got a major problem," Hal says, and proceeds to explain in excruciating detail the technical flaw in the mid-range server Tris sold him several months ago that has prevented it from coming on line properly and has subsequently transformed Integrated's refrigerated warehouse in New Jersey into a vast cavern piled high with rapidly defrosting frozen foods.

"I'm certainly aware of the ramifications," Tris says, using the biggest, most neutral, concern-filled word he can come up with.

"This is ten million dollars of product on the line—what are you going to do about it?"

"Well Hal," he says, mind racing through an algorithm of emergency phone calls he can place to various technical support staff at his company, "I'll get my tech guys in touch with your facility manager within the next thirty minutes."

"Too late! My ass is toast if you don't have someone out here on site in the next fifteen minutes. I've been trying to reach you all night—why don't you answer your goddamn phone?"

That's a very good question, he thinks, eyes scanning the menu, wishing he had the green-bottled beer and the steak already in front of him. His eyes search the room, looking for help to come from somewhere—Leo the waiter perhaps—someone, anyone to get him out of this life of talking people into buying things that he has sullenly trudged through for the past forty-five years. Maggie the hostess is leading her large crowd of anticipated diners to their preferable spot in the center of the restaurant, the excited high notes of their laughter rising above the clink of silverware and glasses as tables are shoved together to accommodate them. A quick, furtive movement in the aquarium catches his eye: there, in the corner, something moved.

At first glance the large dim box seems to be devoid of life, the murky water filtered with bubbles from a hidden pump, glowing with a yellowish light from a lamp that's been latched onto the top rim of the tank. In the lower corners of the tank are two complementary piles of brown that he first assumed were merely accumulated filth. This is where the movement came from. An abrupt, precise wave of a tentacle that stirs a swirl of water and registers the objects squashed into the corners of the tank as lobsters—stacked in a seething, swarming pile of legs and beaks, pincers and eye stalks and fluttering tails that curl and uncurl as one of the creatures struggles to extract itself from the slumbering mound of its brethren. Hal Pope and his warehouse of spoiling food seem very far away now. Tris's thoughts are locked on the brown speckled creature making its way across the floor of the aquarium towards the stack of lobsters on the opposite side, wondering what is going through the tiny brain of this animal, what makes it do what it's doing? Then, suddenly, a bare arm thrusts itself into the tank and reaches for the fellow who singled himself out by emerging from the pile, the hand missing once as he scrabbles away, but catching him with a second swipe, lifting the poor fellow up and out of the water, the limp, segmented carapace of his tail dripping as he's hoisted to his doom.

"Listen, Hal," Tris says, his voice coming from some other compartment of his being, the area he has come to think of as 'auto-pilot,' the part of him that sends the e-mail and checks the voice mail and files the expense report spreadsheets once a week. "I'll get my best guy on it—Teddy Kucic. You met him when we did the installation a few weeks ago." And now the vague promise turns into a lie. "I'm sure I can have him reach you in no time."

Maggie is just as busy as she said she would be. Now she's seating a family of four at a table directly in front of him who look for all the world as if they're here on vacation, the two small children, a boy and a girl, clutching souvenirs the parents bought them at the local museum or zoo or theme park. The father is solicitous of his wife and his two young children, making sure they have what they need—he reaches over to another table and hands the boy a roll of silverware wrapped in a linen napkin. It's clear that this is a special occasion for the family, having steak at a fancy restaurant. Tris's heart swells to think of the planning discussions that must have gone into this choice, the wife perhaps questioning whether it's too much money to spend on a meal the children might not even enjoy, the father insisting that they deserve to eat at least one meal in some place other than a fast-food joint—it will expand the kids' horizons— Tris knows, he can picture every last detail, he has been in these same situations before, two children of his own, raised and sent to college and gone now, leaving him with only memories of long-ago moments such as these. Hal's tiny voice is saying something to Tris from very far away. Instead of listening to him, Tris watches the back of the little girl's head as she tries to read the menu, her

hair parted very precisely down the back of her head, her mother for all the wanting must have taken the time to comb the hair out very carefully as she got the girls ready to come here. The part divides her head into two perfect halves, a line down the back of her head where I can see the pretty pink scalp, the pig tails braided out to either side as she bends her head down. The other one with her hair in curls that dip down over her eyes while she eats the melon.

"Go ahead girls, salt it. This is the way we eat it." Her mother must love them very much, in spite of the wanting. When Tris went away I never had another—never had Tris in that way as a matter of fact. I kept myself whole, I saved myself for you Tris, but you never came back, you never came, and so I kept you in my heart. I kept us together in my heart, and you have always been here with me even though you are still so far away. I kept myself for you all these years, went to work after high school, Father said if you're not going to get a man you have to get a job. Went to work at Grain Dealers Mutual for thirty-eight years, they gave me early retirement when the company was sold, and lived with Karl while he was a minister here, while he stayed here. He came back from Philadelphia and then Dennis died in the war, the Purple Heart is still on the bureau in Karl's room. It will always be there, along with the Bible Karl left me. I have it here and read it every evening.

I never read it straight through or follow what the Sunday teacher says, I flip the book open and see what it has for me today:

Phillip came and told Andrew. Then Andrew and Phillip together went and told Jesus. And Jesus answered them, The time has come for the Son of man to be glorified and exalted. I assure you, most solemnly I tell you, Unless a grain of wheat falls into the earth and dies, it remains just one grain; never becomes more but lives by itself alone. But if it dies, it produces many others and yields a rich harvest. Any one who loves his life loses it. But anyone who hates his life in this world will keep it to life eternal – Whoever has no love for, no concern for, no regard for his life here on earth, but despises it, preserves his life forever and ever.

The car rolls by slowly, big town car color of champagne, big Lincoln with its headlights on against the dusk, slowly rolling and watching, looking for something on this street. The drugs and the women are a problem now, this neighborhood used to be so nice with the tall trees lining both sides of the street and the houses set up on the hills, but now these fellows roll by in their old cars looking for something, looking for trouble.

"Come on girls." Her pigtails flounce in silent reply, turning to look at me, questioning, sensing the fear in my voice. "Let's finish the melon inside."

We go

inside through the front door tonight for a change, Holly wants to make it more of a proper date instead of sneaking into the kitchen from the service entrance at the back. She ignores the cordon of hostesses lined up at the front to stop people and take their names—the wait is typically at least an hour and a half by this time of night. Who knows what they come for? Holly has convinced herself that the food isn't really that good, but you get less of it, so people flock here thinking it must be something special. And it has become somewhat of a scene at the large dimly lit bar in the back of the restaurant: People come here to see and be seen, to show off their cars and their jewelry and their facelifts and boob jobs and trophy wives and mistresses and designer T-shirts and handbags. These fads come and go, however. In six months, the same crowd of social climbers will have determined through some unseen, unspoken mutual decision that the Midtown Grill is no longer the place and some other newly named or freshly opened disco or bistrot or Thai-Cuban gastropub will assume the mantle of hot spot in this prosperous, slightly-behind-the-times Midwestern city. Holly feels a pinch in her chest as she strides through the clattering din of the main dining room: She is one of them, part of the scene. Eyes lock on her as she floats her way towards the bar, taking her in, watching, calculating, assessing—is this someone I know, or someone I should know? What's so special about her? She knows she's being examined like a model strutting down the runway, and she does her best to hold up her end of the bargain even though she's only a single-parent hairdresser who grew up in a farm town twenty miles away. The fullness in her chest grows until she's back at the bar, smothered by the throng of people standing there, safe in her accustomed domain.

She scans behind the bar for Rick, but doesn't see him.

"Hey Charlie!" she calls out, raising her voice against the competing throb of the piped-in technopop music and the mumble of the baseball game on TV. "Where's Rick?"

Charlie gives her a welcoming smile as he slings gin into a tumbler. "Cigarette break." He slides the G and T to a man with slicked-back hair in a business suit and without asking pops open one of the saccharine sweet malt liquor beverages that have become Holly's mainstay over the three weeks since she started seeing Rick and spending as many evenings as she can possibly manage here. She promised herself on the way over that she would play it a little cooler tonight with Rick, not let herself look quite so desperate to see him when she arrived, and she felt that she was all set to go through with the act, but now that she's here and he's not, she feels the need pressing down on her even more acutely, an unbearable weight that must be lifted.

Holly sips on the cool sweet liquid, like drinking the syrup they use to make Sno-cones but laced with alcohol, the benefit being that she can consume three or four of these in rapid succession to quickly get a buzz going. Rick always tries to make her do a shot, but she hates the burning feeling of the raw alcohol going down. This way is much more pleasant, like drinking your desert. The alcohol taste is almost completely hidden.

The man in the suit is looking her over, trying not to appear obvious as he stares down her shirt. She gives him a smile and turns away, peering up at the TV screen where a baseball player tugs at his crotch, waves his bat back and forth peremptorily, and spits. Still no Rick.

She really doesn't want to do this—it is counter to her plan of action for the night—but she circles around the bar with drink in hand and goes into the bright noisy whiteness of the kitchen searching for him. She finds him, standing with his tall lean back to her, his short-cropped black hair thinning on top, gazing out the open back door at the night sky beyond. His form is for her essentially nothing more than a template of a man: the broad shoulders, narrow waist, small bottom, and lean legs evoke a rush of all the old feelings, an aching sick need that wells up from a tight precious sanctuary within her. The thinning hair, the bald spot, is a trigger too: He is older. She needs him, has something to give him, so she can connect with him.

She must make him want her. And so, without a word of warning, she silently comes up behind him and wraps her arms around him, holding on. Holding on

tight to my hand again, the youngest one is afraid as I go to the door. I shouldn't even answer it. Maybe Tassie Jensen came by again to talk, maybe Dolores or one of the Salgados, could be anyone, but that car was watching us, slowed down to take a look in our direction, inspecting as it went past. There's another series of raps on the window of the door, slow and careful and precise, determined and patient, not wanting much to intrude, just letting us know he is here. I can tell it is a man's knock, the weight of it heavier, more direct, slow, careful, and precise, letting us know he is

here

by the elevators, Tris punches the button with the arrow pointing up and waits, the meal done, the twelve ounces of beef sitting heavy in his stomach, the acidic flavor of Hal Pope's anger and disappointment still settling over his palate, mingling with the aftertaste of the beer from the green bottle. The meal was essentially ruined by a series of unpleasant and disjointed phone calls to track down a technician within short driving distance of the New Jersey plant to deal with the meltdown on site, and now the gurgling water from the fountain that dominates the hotel lobby seems to flow through him like time passing, moments of his life trickling away, lost, never to be recaptured again.

He wonders why it's taking so long for the elevator to arrive, and his impatience makes him punch the Up button again, as if pressing the button another time will make the elevator come sooner. He stares at the brushed metal doors in front of him, willing them to open, when he sees out of the corner of his eye a woman walk up to the farthest of the four elevators and go in. This doesn't make sense—the arrow is supposed to blink off when an elevator arrives—but now he glances down at the button as he hurries to the far doors and sees that it is indeed dark. He senses that the doors will soon close on him and he'll be left behind. The feeling of running late, being slightly behind the curve, descends upon him again, a brief flutter in his chest like a bird landing on a power line. He launches himself towards the rapidly closing doors and thrusts a foot and an arm in just before they close. It seems as if the doors will clamp down on him with a crushing force, and he braces for the hit. Somehow, though, the doors stop short with a jerking clunk. The woman has put her arm in front of them just as he leaps in, triggering the automatic stop mechanism. The doors suddenly slide all the way open again, and Tris pulls himself up short, slowing down the momentum of his leap and trying to maintain a semblance of grace as he steps lightly into the dim glass box and swivels around to get a look at his savior.

She's tall, slim, surprisingly pretty. Thick reddish brown hair straight past her shoulders, a color that makes Tris think of a fox's tail. She's wearing business clothes: form-fitting slacks and a russet-brown jacket cut above the waist. The doors stand completely ajar for a few seconds now, dumbly awaiting any further passengers who might choose to board, and Tris presses 18, the button for his floor. Tris smiles at the woman and notices that she doesn't press another button, as the doors slither shut and the floor starts to lift, the sensation of rising up making it seem for a transitory instant as if he is floating there in the box with her.

Only 18 is lit.

For several seconds the elevator passes through a gaping interval where the only view out of the three glass walls away from the doors is a black shaft of darkness, as if instead of going up he is descending deep into the earth. Instinctively, both Tris and the woman stand facing the doors at the front of the elevator, and Tris politely keeps his gaze focused on the bank of thirty or so buttons, staring at the glowing 18. Then, a sudden wash of light floods the box and both of them irresistibly turn to face the back of the elevator as it soars above the vast open space of the lobby. Having been buried in darkness, they are now rocketing up to heaven. The hotel is one of those that has been designed around an atrium—Tris can see the floors stacked one on top of the other as they swiftly rise over the fountain and the potted trees and lobby where people walking here and there dwindle to the size of ants. The woman surprises him by talking.

"I don't like these elevators that you can see out of. It's such a long way to fall."

Neither does Tris. As a matter of fact, this glass box being hoisted into the air is one of the least pleasant places he could find himself in. His claustrophobia is only slightly offset by the sense of open space that the glass walls afford, and that benefit is marred by the fact that he is also profoundly afraid of heights, but usually when he's in a high, open place such as the corridors of this hotel. The combination of being in an enclosed place that's also soaring up to the sky engenders a feeling of floating, drifting nausea, the dinner he just ate churning like a chunk of molten lead within him.

"I'd rather fall," Tris says airily, "than be trapped inside here."

"It wouldn't be bad, if you had the right person with you."

Tris wonders at first if he's heard her correctly, then checks himself to see if he has not misinterpreted the meaning implied by her remark. She must be twenty years younger than him, but he has been told by many people that he looks much younger than his age. And after forty, he thinks, who cares? We're all damaged goods, even this woman, soon to be no use to any one, not even ourselves. Tris allows himself to glance at her, and she returns his look with a smile that is dazzling, gorgeous. His first impression was correct: she is young, attractive, and flirting with him. His mind spins through the possibilities that unfurl from her smile, a businesswoman traveling for work like him, lonely, perhaps single or divorced, looking for some excitement where the opportunity presents itself. Discreetly, he places his left hand, the one with the ring on it, in his pocket, hoping she hasn't already noticed. Yet even in doing so, a wave of conflicting images ripples through his head—his wife's number scrolling across the phone, this woman standing naked in his hotel room, the gently twisting, glowing tape measure that haunted him earlier in the evening, the lone scrabbling lobster being snatched from its tank. Tris turns away from the yawning

41

chasm outside the glass box to face the doors again, anticipating his stop, and she turns with him.

Staring straight ahead, he catches a blurred reflection of himself from the burnished metal doors. He can make out only the faintest impression of a nose, a mouth, a shock of black hair, but no eyes; only the glinting of light from the rims of his glasses. The digital readout above the doors flashes in rhythm, 14...15...16...17, as if counting his heartbeats, then pauses an extra long moment on 17 as the lifting force decelerates, finally lurching to a stop on 18. The doors swoosh open and a bright, quiet anteroom awaits him, empty hallways to either side, no one watching, no one here to witness what is happening. An invitation to do whatever he decides.

As is customary at these hotels, the front desk for some reason has given him two keys when he checked in. Tris finds this practice vaguely annoying, because he typically keeps his room key in his wallet and he doesn't like leaving the extra key lying around where the maids or service people can get it—an irrational fear; they're already in your room if they can take it from your desk. Still, just to be safe, he always puts both keys in his wallet, the two plastic cards making it extra thick and bulky in his pocket. Tris allows the woman to step out of the elevator ahead of him, and as she does so, he deftly retrieves one of the room keys. Then there is a moment when she is just in front of him, as they both step into the quiet vestibule together, when he can smell her fox-colored hair only inches from his face and peer down her spine to the tight slacks that cling to the curve of her bottom.

She turns to face him, her lips parted by something she's already planning to say, but the key card he extends to her makes the word stop coming and her mouth twist into a smile. She's slightly startled by what he has done, her eyes blinking once, twice, but she doesn't hesitate—she opens her hand to accept the key. As he hands it to her, he has the impression that he is fulfilling some obligation of polite courtesy that a man must extend to a woman in this particular situation—that, having been conjoined by fate inside the same tight, enclosed space and having received the gift of the woman's flirting words and smile, he is duty-bound to invite her back to his room in order to avoid appearing rude. But even as she takes the key, Tris's mind is performing a back flip at the apex of its precipitous dive from this height of presumption. All the old rules and proscriptions, admonitions and commandments he has absorbed since his earliest days combine to form a chorus of guilt that says: *How can you do this? You have never been unfaithful to your wife. You are a good person.* In the backwash of the next heartbeat, his mind has achieved a nimble solution and his smile is tinged with self-righteous regret as he says, "I need to make a couple of phone calls, but come by in a few minutes if you'd like to join me for a drink. I'm in 1836," he says, completing the gesture, carrying out all his duties, knowing full well that he has given her the wrong room

number of reasons to keep this man out of the house, a stranger with these girls here. Even as the door is opening and he steps in, the smell of aftershave, cologne, a wave of bristly whiskers shorn and perfumed, a sweet sour smell of flowers dying. His face is dark, a shadow hangs upon his smile, his crooked teeth. He says "Look who's here, hello Zoe," even as the girls come closer, but still they stay away. They know him, know he is someone to make them not frightened, but only give him a shy smile. He is a remembered stranger.

"Come here girls and give me a big hug."

They go, but only Zoe goes first with short small steps. He stoops down and brings her to his chest, dressed in a pair of blue jeans and a plaid shirt, a country gentleman in for a visit, but how did he know? The bells of St. Monica sound out loud from across the block: one, two, three times, the stroke of the big iron bell, we used to run to the tower and watch it toll back and forth, its slow swinging like being in the hammock back and forth, it seemed to pause at the top of each end of the swing and hang there, slow and without effort, when you get to the top the earth will pull you back down. The big iron tongue clanging seven, eight, nine, it is nine already, the August light goes too soon. The youngest girl releases herself from him and the oldest one steps forward, leans in, and lets herself be held by small degrees. He reaches over and around her shoulders and pulls her close, and still she shies away.

"I came to see you girls, stopped by for a visit," he says, arching his back to its full height again. "I brought you something from the stables. See," he says, and hands her a rusted brown horseshoe. "I know you like horses."

The youngest one turns away and says, "I want to go out to the swing again, can we?"

It is only just outside, only the bells have stopped tolling, and the last fragment of their sound is still sending across the houses and trees, sending its note to you, its solemn hollow note says I am still here, I will always be here with you, we will always be together. The rope was frayed at the end when you pulled it and nothing happened, too heavy, then we both jumped up and grabbed on as high as we could

fall down in a heap of writhing lust for each other right here in the damp alley behind the kitchen but that would not be right, not keeping with the plan for tonight, Holly thinks, what has happened to the plan? She was going to be in control tonight, in control of the cruel wanting need she has, but here she is with a man in her arms pressing her self against him, running her hands up his back, his broad strong back, rubbing her breasts against him. He bends to her and puts his mouth on her. His hands are on her ass, finding their way there, and she must get it under control. She says, "No, wait," and pulls her self away from him. "Not here."

She can make herself wait for him, she must prove it, to herself. She will wait for him until midnight or later, until after he closes. It is a test she must not fail, she is trying to gain control of her self, to push away the latticework of her need, to crawl out from inside it.

"Isn't there someplace we can go?" he says, his voice low, nearly a whisper. "I have a few minutes. They can handle it while I'm gone."

Through the filminess of her dress, he latches on with two fingers to the taut elastic of her panties and drags it up her bottom, like pulling a cord that turns on the electricity to a certain finely tuned instrument. Her mind is swept by a cold blankness that clarifies her thinking. She grabs his hand and removes it from her, then leads him down the alley, damp with humid night air and the dull resonance of reverberating bass notes seeping from the bars and nightclubs. One of the clubs actually has its main entrance on the alley, a bright doorway where a cluster of young drunks staggers beneath a neon sign that flashes THE CASBAH. A bald, puffy-looking bouncer in a leather jacket calls out to them as they hurry past.

"Fifty cent pitchers and two dollar shots! No cover for the lady."

Holly has been in the Casbah before, trolling. Now that she thinks about it, she may have met Rick there—it's only been three weeks, but it seems like a very long time ago. She tugs on his hand to make sure he knows not to go in. There are iron bars on the windows of the buildings that back onto the alley. A scrawl of graffiti mars the wall of one of them, an illegible design that looks like a group of letters but might also be a pitchfork topped with a crown. There are more people here, mostly young, in their teens and twenties, packs of them crowding the sidewalk, girls outnumbering boys. Holly thinks of them as predators, searching, seeking, their laughter somehow sinister. At the light where they wait to cross the street, a huddle of girls in jeans and tube tops surrounds a woman in a white wedding dress, complete with headpiece and a long, gauzy train. The light changes and the women lurch into the busy street, laughing, as they struggle to avoid the idling cars and keep the train of the dress off the pavement.

"I think I know them," Rick says, glancing over his shoulder. "It's Mitzi Kluger's bachlorette party."

Holly doesn't know them—doesn't want to know them. The red door to her shop is there, ahead of them, a few feet away. She digs the keys out of her purse, fumbles for the one that opens the shop. She tries to jam it into the hole, misses in her hurry, gouging the red paint. Tries again and feels it slot in, tongues of grooved metal interlocking. Turns the key and they are inside, the echoing chamber of the stairway leading to the second-floor shop lit only by the diffuse light of the moon reflected through broad panes of glass high above them. She leads them up quickly, feels his face a few steps behind her, seeking, directly at the level of her thighs. With the moon bouncing around the many mirrored surfaces of the salon, there is enough light to make their way. She has spent so many hours of her life here, she could lead them even if there were only darkness. She takes him to her station, her sanctuary, the place where she performs her best work. They have screwed in the back seats of cars, against the wall of a building in the alley, in his apartment, and once on the hard dry dirt of a jogging path in a city park, but this is the best yet; leading him to her sanctuary. At first she thinks of the chair in which her customers sit to have their hair cut, then she has a better idea: The chair where she washes their hair tips all the way back.

She stands next to the sink, turns to face him.

"Wait . . . " she says, trying it out, testing it, her mind still wanting to put it off a moment longer.

He grabs her by the wrists and pins the small of her back against the edge of the table that holds her brushes and combs, presses her down onto it, scattering the framed pictures of the girls to the floor. She struggles against him, lifts her knee into his groin and pushes him away. In the small opening this creates, she slips out from under him, yanks her arm loose, feels his fingernails claw at her skin, and even as she twirls away from him, he latches on to her

hand and leads me out past the snap dragons and the azaleas, the cone flowers and the stone dish of the bird bath, all faded pale in the new shadows of the moon, their colors dim and washed away, the whirring of the cicadas shimmering over the traffic sounds, the swish of the cars going by and the calls of the Mexicans out in the street singing their dancing words to each other. The bench of the swing holds us, her small body tucked against mine.

"Higher," she says, "make it go higher." We kick, kick at the back of the arc, and the wind races through our ears, *down in the valley, valley so low,* we sang, *hang your head over, hear the wind blow.* We sang this Tris, our legs kicking up higher, higher. *If you don't love me, love whom you please, throw your arms round me, give my heart*

ease

back into the chair, feeling it slide down beneath her, tilting her head back onto the smooth lip of the sink, the U-shaped channel where the neck is supposed to go, like putting her head into a type of harness. Now he has her there, wrists pinioned against the arms of the chair, he throws his weight on top of her, the bulk of his chest pressing her down. His mouth is seeking, she feels his lips against her collarbone, then further down, to the flattened exposed flesh of her right breast. He always goes for the right one first; she arches her back to meet him. In the basement office her stepfather led her, said *I have something to show you.* His secret place, his sanctuary. And he opened the drawer of his metal Sears desk, brought out a small leather-bound book. Red. Its cover was bright red with gold lettering embossed into the spine, like a holy book. Rick is pulling her blouse off now, she tilts herself up in the chair and complies, undoing the bra, she helps him, his hands fiddling with the latches, tangled up with hers. The pages he flipped through in no particular hurry, not especially eager, like a lesson in school. He was going to show her something, and she knew it was somehow not right, a vibration in the air between them, hanging there, like two dissonant notes in a chord on the piano. But she wanted so much to please him, she leaned over his shoulder and there—on the glossy slick page of the book, a photograph in black and white. He paused and they saw it together, without comment, he turned the next page and another photo, he said *This is what it looks like, have you ever seen it before,* as if he were telling her a story. And still she trusted

him to be there inside the house alone with the other girl, they seem to know him, he said I brought you something from the stables, the horseshoe rusty and brown. I came to see you girls, stopped by for a visit. The youngest one turned away. She says, "Look at the moon," and

49

it's still rising past the roof of the house, it swings up and away, then down and back towards us again. "Look at the moon." Almost full, a bright orange ball looming up in the sky, not a harvest moon yet. What do they call a full moon in August, is it a harvest moon? Up and away it swings, then down and back it approaches us, then pulls away. The feeder and birdbath are swathed in yellow light, now more golden than before. The flowers in Elmer's bed shimmer in the light. The other girl has been inside some time now, his crooked teeth and the sweet sour smell of his cologne. "Honey, let's stop now, it's getting late. We better go

inside her, he pushes himself close and her legs go wider, knocking against the hard metal arms of the chair, she feels her self locked into place beneath him, underneath him, within him, she rocks her back up to meet him. They are together now, at last, she has given her self to him, the bones at the base of her skull knocking against the hard ceramic lip of the sink, she feels as if she is pouring her self up out of this basin into him. There is nothing more she can do for him, she is giving all that she has to give and when he closed the red book with the startling odd pictures in it he took her hand and placed it where it wasn't supposed to be, where she never should have

left

that girl inside the house with him alone, what was I thinking? I'm an old maid who has no understanding of the world, only my own little slice of it, my own little tunnel, a cave I live in, my house, my garden, and the shame of it is I have chosen this way, this enclosure, this structure I have built around myself like a framework of steel that sustains me, holds me together. My memories, my visions hold me together. I have nobody but you. The girl tries to go ahead of me, but I hold onto her hand and keep her beside me. We go up the steps, and I pull open the screen door, and the moonlight

bounces off the mirror beyond his shoulder, bounces its golden light at her as she loses her self within him, as the red book goes away for a moment it is all washed away, all the guilt and shame and anguish he bestowed upon her, all the fear wrapped up in her need to please the person who was supposed to take care of her, all wound up in a distortion like the weird tremors of light that move back and forth, back and forth from the mirror, a secret a child knows but can never say. Her head bangs hard against the ceramic lip of the sink, pounding the pain out of her, yet even so the smell of him flooding back to her mouth, smell of fish and wet hay flooding her

way through the kitchen, the dishes not done, the sauerkraut still in the can, past the door to the dining room where there is no sound. I am missing my shows tonight for these girls. Usually the sound of the television fills the house, keeps the darkness outside, but nothing now. The room is dark except for the rectangle of light that comes from the living room, illuminating the breakfront.

"Wait," I say to the girl in a whisper. I put my hand out to the wall to feel it, to hold me steady. The wallpaper is smooth and cool. I tell her with the force of my other hand to stop a

51

moment, stay behind me, then I peer my head around the doorway into the living room.

They are sitting on the couch, a book open in front of them, a book he must have brought. I have no book in there but the Bible Karl gave me, and that is not a story book or a Bible either, then it is there like an object out of place, condemned to never fit, his hand where it should not be placed in such a matter-of-fact way she sits there transfixed, her whole body pinned down by it, that awful flat hand in the one place in all the earth where it should never be, and the only thing to do is to reach for the nearest thing I can find. I let go of the girl. The closest thing is the vase, the beautiful vase, grab it by the handle and hurl it through the door across the room. It sails so fast and misses, striking the wall above his head. His head dips down automatically to protect itself, the one thing in this house that doesn't need protecting. It hits the wall and shatters, it flies into a bright star of fragments and the moment is

broken,   lying

with him on top of her still, her skull a precious vessel will be broken if he keeps going this way, the small compartment that holds the giant ball of her self will be

broken never one whole

together

again he finds himself lying awake on the king bed with the television on, the sound turned down low, staring up at the ceiling and thinking about the woman on the elevator, the woman who offered herself to him, whom he deceived and could not offer himself to. He is safe here, always taking the

CHRIS KATSAROPOULOS

safest way out, the easiest way, the cleanest way out. Yet he wonders what has happened: Did she try to come and find him? Did she go back to her room first or wait a moment in the vestibule and follow him down the corridor and see him go into his room—not the room he told her. A moment of panic which swiftly converts itself into a perverse wave of hope: Perhaps she will come by and knock on the door, any second now. Of course she will. The way she smiled at him in the elevator, *it wouldn't be bad, if you had the right person with you.* Of course she will—she wants him, loves him, in her mind in the elevator while he was still thinking about the floating lead-like feeling of the dinner in his stomach, she was entertaining images of the two of them trapped in the box together taking each other's clothes off and having sex.

Now he wants her to come to his door and knock, he wills her to. This is the kind of fantasy Tris has read about in pornographic magazines, the kind of brief set up shot they use to get the action going in the pay-per-view movies he sometimes samples as a diversion to sway himself to sleep in these nameless hotel rooms he inhabits. And yet, he is so pilgrimatically programmed for the straight and narrow path that he turned this lovely woman away, he knowingly denied himself the opportunity to enjoy this beautiful woman's body, and it fills him with regret.

Tris imagines what the woman is doing now—perhaps she's trying to figure out a way to find him. His only hope is that she would have tried other doors, knocking on the ones nearby the

53

one he told her. Perhaps she's simply allowing plenty of time for him to make his calls.

Tris presses himself up off the bed and pads over to the door, looking out through the peephole. The hallway is empty, quiet. The view through the tiny opening seems to expand into a kind of rounded off perspective, the walls in one direction absurdly huge in the middle of his view and then shrinking down to a narrowing middle distance in which a few of the other doors down the hall are bent into a strange curving shape, and finally collapsing in the far distance to a kind of nothingness, an obscure edge. The view is also distorted by seeing it with only one eye, giving it a flatness that seems to compress everything towards him, depriving it of depth. His eyes blink at the effort of seeing this way, trying to maintain focus. He pulls his head back for a second, then tries again, aligning his right eye, the dominant one, to the hole, looking first left and then right down the hallway. Across the hall, an opposing door is large and almost undisturbed by the peculiar curvature that shapes the rest of the hall. Tris imagines that in some way this aperture is showing him the present moment straight ahead, with the past narrowing down towards the left and the future shrinking down to the right, both directions of the hallway empty and increasingly distant and unclear.

He has an idea—for a split second it seems like a good one. Maybe he can call the front desk and somehow reach her. But even as he backs away from the peephole, he realizes this is absurd. He doesn't know her name or her room number—all he knows is that she's on the eighteenth floor, and maybe even that is not true. Perhaps she just followed him to the floor he is on by not pressing another floor in the elevator. Still, he has nothing better to do. He goes to the phone and dials the hotel operator, letting it ring a long time before a man with what sounds like an Arabic accent picks up, carefully pronouncing the hotel's pretentious marketing phrase.

"It's a wonderful night at the Windsor. How may I help you?"

Tris frames the words in his head, deciding the best way to ask this, thinking, I'm trying to reach a woman on the eighteenth floor.

"Hello?" the Arab says, pinching the o sound into more of a rising oo. "How may I help you?"

Tris stays on the line a moment longer, then calmly puts the phone in its cradle without saying a word.

Back on the bed, Tris lies there, staring at the ceiling, and he knows now that the woman is not coming. Another opportunity lost. Another door not opened. And here he is, safe, secure in his cell. His mind slowly spins back to other situations such as this over the years, other women he turned away in favor of the confines of his marriage. He ticks them off in his head, working backwards one by one, making a list. The woman from the church Bible study group who phoned one day a year or two ago, sounding surprised to reach him, asking if she could come by to drop something off, a parcel for the outreach ministry, knowing full well he was alone and Laura was out of town, visiting her sister in Tulsa. There was the co-worker from the home office, confiding to him over drinks at a cocktail lounge in Chicago that she didn't mind being married—she loved her husband—but she missed the wild, wanton sex she used to have with strangers.

There was the neighbor long ago when he was first married, who used to flirt shamelessly with him, dropping hints every now and then that she was available if he wanted her. Tris ticks off their names in his head, a dozen or more—too many to count really—some of them nameless, like the woman tonight, nothing more than blurry memories, each of them turned away through a combination of fear and an overriding desire to stay in the right. And this brings him back to the first one, whose name he will never forget, so long ago it seems like another person's life. Fifty or sixty years ago it was. Whatever happened to Amelia?

The ceiling above his head is too low, eight feet at most, and the ceiling tiles seem to be shifting slightly, pressing down on him. The acoustic tiles are filled with thousands of little holes to absorb the sound, a dizzying random configuration like black stars in a white sky. Tris stares at these holes as they move, shift. There is something about them, one tile separated from the next by an aluminum strip. And then he sees it, in the first tile, directly above his head: A repetition. There is a certain pattern, a kind of pinwheel arc aligning one sequence of holes, like the arm of a galaxy, and as he lifts his head to look closer he sees it again, several inches away from the first, the same swirling pattern of holes.

He looks at other sections of the tile and he can see different alignments, different sizes and shapes of holes, and as his eye moves across the tile he recognizes other recurrences, other places where certain arrangements reappear. For an instant, it's as if he's seeing down into the sky and the wide expanse of nothingness he fell into earlier is back. The patterns are all evident—they were there all along, but his mind wasn't attuned to this level of detail. He remembers reading something in a magazine article, something that seemed strange at the time, but makes perfect sense now. The article said that a scientist in eastern Europe, a mathematician most likely or a physicist, was debunking all the recent research about chaos and randomness. This man said there is no such thing as randomness—nothing is random. There is a pattern—a design—for everything: weather, the forking of a tree's branches, the shapes of clouds, constellations of stars. It's just that the patterns are at a level of complexity our brains cannot possibly process, so we see them as random. And Tris imagines now a machine in a factory somewhere—a plant that may well be using one of his computer systems—punching a precise pattern of holes into thousands upon thousands of acoustic tiles, diligently, mindlessly repeating the same sequence of holes over and over again.

CR

"GOODBYE ENRIQUE."

"Where you going?" he says, sitting on the other side of the porch, chewing seeds on Elmer's porch, in the metal chair where Elmer used to sit.

"Going downtown," I say, not telling him everything. "Going to do some shopping." He doesn't need to know exactly where I'm going. "I won't be back until late." All morning the smell of that man was in the house, in the front room, the smell of his after shave cologne, the same color as his champagne car. Down the steps, careful now, take each one sideways, both feet on one, then the next one, then both feet on the next. They seem to be steeper now through the gate in the fence, his champagne car parked right here in front, but he hurried out didn't he when I broke the porcelain vase, when I threw it at him he scurried off right away. He didn't say a word of goodbye to those girls, those precious

girls, I want you to stop making that noise—this instant!" Holly's head pounds as she turns slowly, gingerly, to look at the clock on the table across the room. It seems to be a great distance from her. She has to squint to make out the position of the absurdly ornamental hands, each composed of a flowing scrollwork so complex that it is difficult to tell the difference between the big hand and the small hand. Three-thirty it seems to be saying—can it be? Where has the day gone? Lying on the couch all morning with a blanket over her and the frantic gibbering of the Saturday morning cartoons, she had to call in sick again, her head swimming as if it has been submerged in a vast vat of liquid teeming with muffled noises, a throb of pain at the back of her skull any time she turns her head. Saturday, her biggest day of the week, seven customers canceled and all because of Rick. No, not Rick. She knows it was her own overweening need for him, her own baseless hunger that got her into this again.

"Turn off the TV Jenny," she says. "You've had it on all day." Beyond the crest of a fold in the blanket that covers her, the screen flickers with frenzied images. Jenny ignores her mother for a moment and Zoe sits beside her Indian-style on the living room floor of the small apartment, fumbling with something in her hands.

"I said turn it off, and I *mean* it."

She really shouldn't yell at them, the effort of opening her mouth that wide and expelling the words sends a spasm of pain up the back of her head. Jenny looks around at her mother, to see if she's really serious, and Holly returns the look. Then Holly closes her eyes for a moment and lets her head sink into the pillow, inhaling and then releasing a deep breath. Let them watch if they want to, she thinks. The reddish-orange afterimage of the screen glows on the backs of her eyelids, floats there and contorts into a lozenge of fading brilliance. Let them watch. Why should she be so hard on them after she made them stay at the old lady's house last night and now here they are stuck in the apartment with her all day today. Jenny was so good, getting bowls of cereal for Zoe and herself this morning, opening a can of tomato soup with the electric can opener and heating it for their lunch. Jenny must think her mother is a drunk—she knows about it now, they teach them about drugs, and cigarettes, and drinking in school. Maybe sex too, in fifth or sixth grade. Or maybe that's next year. Zoe just thinks that she's sick all the time, but this time is more than a hangover. The back of her head is pounding, where it slammed into the lip of the sink. And then, as she lies there with her eyes closed, drinking in the grey darkness, the sound of the TV goes away.

"Oh . . . " she says, with her eyes still closed. "Thank you Jenny."

She could drift off into sleep again in the quiet. The girls she hears as soft rustling sounds, getting up from the floor, moving closer.

"It was me," Zoe says, letting her know she's a helper too.

Holly's eyes open slightly, revealing harsh trapezoids of sunlight slanting in past the floor-to-ceiling vertical blinds that shield the sliding doors to the balcony. Now the girls have nothing to do. Jenny sits on the floor, staring at the TV screen as if it still emits some form of entertainment for her. Maybe she's waiting for her mother to fall asleep again so she can turn it back on. Zoe walks past the couch towards the small dining area and the galley kitchen—getting a snack. When they're not watching TV, Holly thinks, they eat.

"Why don't you go outside," Holly says, "and play. It's nice out."

"Play what?" Jenny says. She's reached the age where all her answers assume the form of a challenge, an impertinent dig at Holly's authority. Holly can think of any number of things to play, games she used to play with kids in the neighborhood when she was young, running loose for hours, but her head is throbbing so much that the words cannot form, the names of those simple games seem to elude her, and even if she could remember, they don't live in the same kind of neighborhood she did, the residents of the apartment complex are transient, mostly young singles or older retired couples on fixed incomes. There is a small playground in the courtyard behind their building, but the few kids who are around tend to stay inside, their parents wary of letting them go out on their own. As Zoe goes by, Holly notices something in her hand, the thing she was fiddling with on the floor.

"What's that?" she says, raising her arm weakly from under the blanket to gesture at it.

Zoe keeps going to the kitchen but answers after a moment, her voice difficult to hear from behind the door of the cabinet where the snacks are kept. "Nothing," she says, which means nothing important. "Something I found. At the old lady's house."

Zoe comes back to the living room with a box of crackers, the kind that are shaped like fish.

"Let me see," Holly says, and she reaches her hand out to show her she wants it. Zoe stops and looks at Jenny, as if she's asking for her sister's permission. At times it seems as if Zoe has two mothers, as if Jenny has assumed the role of a second parent, filling the void, looking out for Zoe and doling out discipline in Holly's absence, relishing the role of being the oldest. Jenny keeps staring at the screen, ignoring them both.

Reluctantly, Zoe's hand extends the object to her mother, drops it in Holly's open palm.

It hits her ring—the ring on her right hand—with a dull plink. It looks like a piece of broken of pottery, a white curved shard of ceramic slightly larger than Holly's palm. She brings it close to her face and examines it, rotating it to view the jagged edges. It is roughly the shape of a triangle, curved, concave, the sunlight glancing off the shiny face of it. She brushes the ball of her thumb along one of the edges to feel the grainy texture, chalky almost, as opposed to the smooth milk-white face of it. One vertex of the triangle is particularly acute, a point so sharp it could cut.

"Where did you get this?"

Zoe hovers close, eager to retrieve her treasure. "I found it," she says again. "At the old lady's house."

Yes, Holly thinks. I know that. She remembers now that Zoe already told her.

"Looks like something broke."

Zoe glances over at Jenny again, and Jenny is staring at the fragment of porcelain now, watching intently.

"Go on," Holly says. "Tell me. Did you break something there?" Holly can see that something happened, something the girls don't want her to know about. Then, an image flashes in her head and she knows exactly where this came from. She presses the issue.

"I know what this is—I saw it when I was there. The vase from the dining room. The pitcher."

Jenny stands up now, rising to her sister's defense, or ready to plead her case. But Zoe speaks first.

"I did it," she says, her voice tightening in anticipation of a punishment. "I was throwing a ball and it hit the pitcher and broke it." Jenny is watching her closely, as if they have discussed this already, what they would say if their mother found out. "I was throwing the ball to Jenny and she missed and it hit the wall and broke it."

Jenny leans back a little and says, "The old lady was mad. We were surprised she didn't tell you."

"No, she didn't. It was very late."

"She was very mad at Grandpa Steve," Zoe says. She looks at Jenny and realizes she has said too much.

Holly sits up on the couch, raising her head too fast. She closes her eyes and lets the surge of pain crawl up the back of her skull from her neck. And riding along with the pain, flooding her head with the pain, is the smell of him, smell of fish and wet hay, followed by a rapid succession of images—scenes she must blot out—tactile sensations, tastes, a fullness inside her, all things she must twist and turn away. And other things. Her stepfather riding up to her on horseback on the three-acre farm where she spent her late childhood; beaming with pride as he rode towards the house on the colt he had just bought. It must have been only a few days after they arrived at the house in the country: She loved exploring the barn, watching the cats that came with the place sneak around hunting mice. And another thing that fills her aching head: her first father, her real father, arriving home from work at the plant, tired, his hair matted with sweat, head down, but still happy to see her, his oldest daughter—maybe five or six—who had waited at the top of the stairs of their city apartment for him to come home. All tangled up together. Why didn't the old lady tell

her anything, not going to now either, not going to call her on the phone. How could I now—do you know what that man did to your daughter? And if you knew about him before why didn't you tell me about him? I have shut off my life to others in the years since you left, Tris. I have narrowed my self down to a winnowing old maid, sifting out any others who could harm me. I keep them all at arm's length, and even this woman I tried to help I have hurt. I don't know enough about the world and its ways to not end up hurt by another or hurting another. I am a barren seed going about my business, blown by the wind, but never doing any good any more.

The sidewalk marches on my feet beneath me, and here are the steps to the old library. We used to be afraid of the statues of boys with hats on crouched above the doors as you enter, as if they hold up the roof of the building with books in their hands, smiling down like gargoyles. We had to get past them up the stairs. This is one place that has not changed all that much since you were here, the garden and my house and the library are just as you would remember, the same warm oaky feeling, smell of warm sun on the pale wooden floor and books slightly musty. The only difference is they took out a lot of books to make way for the computers, but all of the machines are being used by young black boys not reading or looking for books, they're all playing games with very quiet muffled sounds, shooting space creatures or racing cars. They shouldn't let them use the computers for that. One of them says, "This game is stupid, I'm finding me another one."

The boy pushes back from the screen, and quickly I go over and claim his chair. He looks at me as if he didn't want to give it up after all—or give it up to an old white woman like me, but pay him no mind. Once I plant myself in the chair still warm from his young body, the machine is mine for as long as I need. For as long as I needed you, and still you never came, you never came back. Was it really so bad what Louise said about us, what Father said about us. Was it really so bad that you had to fall from the uppermost edge of the hammock, fall from the edge of the bed in the front room, fall from the top of the tower. We both jumped up and grabbed on as high as we could.

The keys are shadowed with dirt, the beige plastic rimmed by the built-up remnants of many peoples' fingertips typing their messages, sending them into the air. I unfold the paper with the address to type. I can still type seventy words a minute, arthritis or not, the fingers never forget the positions of the keys, the relationships between them. The pictures on the screen change in an instant and the new page comes up, the one I need. *Horace Mann High School Class of 1957 Reunion, Saturday August 11, 2007. We were the lucky ones. We saw the old, yet are living long enough to see the new. Please join us at the Lyceum Theater for dinner, dancing, and a night of memories of dear Horace Mann.*

The screen flickers a bit, difficult to read without glasses, but I'm not bringing them today. You will see me with my hair looking good in its new cut and no glasses, looking as good as a lonely old woman like me possibly can. I have to see if you are coming. One more time I want to see you, at least I think I do.

In *Guest List,* all the names of the people we knew, the ones we admired and the ones we despised, arranged by alphabet. Here it is, like a magic spell, your name on the screen, a pair of words that will always go together and weave a twisting, teasing torment over me: *Tristan Holloway,* with an address and phone number, *5792 Brookshire Lane, Walnut Creek, California.* I always knew you were headed for big things, living in a California desert place with a pool in the back. You must have made your fortune as an artist or an architect, you must have done so well, but it's impossible to tell much more. Is there any way to tell if you are married? Nothing more than a name, an address, and a number to call. And in the line for RSVP, it says *No Response.*

The pencil in my hand is trembling and the numbers on the screen are flickering, they dance and blur. My old eyes are watery. I have to squint to see clearly, but I have it now on the printout, the number that will reach you. You must have built many buildings, I can feel it, but not a tall tower. Instead, something broad and vast and modern, bristling with activity. I can call from the main desk, I know the man there, and he will let me, after one last look at your name on the flickering

screen on the back of the seat in front of him is showing an animated demonstration of a passenger reaching over his head and strapping an oxygen mask over his face. The flight attendants never do the pre-flight instructions now, they realized that no one ever listens anyway, so someone at the headquarters of the airline, some accountant or human efficiency expert, calculated that they would save a certain amount each year if they invested in making this animated video instead of training hundreds of flight attendants what to say and how to say it.

With a hasty flash of whiteness, the screen blinks off, followed by the swooshing logo of the airline, which is then replaced by a cable news network that offers a summary of the day's top stories. The anchor woman on the screen is beautiful, so appealing it is almost painful to look at her. Tris wonders what it must be like for someone to be this attractive, to know that everyone who looks at you is thinking the same thing, is knocked off their feet by your looks. Her auburn hair is swept to one side of her face, a lock of it that's lighter in color just grazing the edge of her eyebrow and framing her astonishing green eyes—and she is not entirely young; that's what really gets him. She must be at least thirty-five. There is a trace of a laugh line—just a trace—at one corner of her lips as she talks, this barely evident imperfection only serving to intensify the marvel of her beauty.

The news happens fast on this network—they have to cover everything in half an hour. As the beautiful green-eyed woman speaks, a grainy videoclip overtakes the screen: A mountainous region in Asia somewhere, loose groups of people standing in the open air swaddled in ragged robes and towel-like headdress, men and women alike. They appear to be wandering aimlessly, and in the background Tris can see that their simple houses have been reduced to rubble. The woman is back for an instant, her dress a shade of green to match her eyes, describing the devastation wrought by the massive earthquake. Then, quickly, a short cut of a child's bloodied body lying in the ruins. And Tris notices for the first time that there is a black rectangle at the bottom of the screen filled with white letters—the closed captioning they provide now for deaf people to receive the bad news too.

Thankfully, the screen returns to the anchor woman, and Tris sees that she is so lovely that she can't help but speak with the trace of a smile on her lips, even as she recites the full dimensions of the catastrophe and outlines the impending aftermath of displacement and disease. The letters in the black box beneath her march on, but the words must be in some sort of foreign language—they don't match what the woman is saying. WEASLDK FNADUK AWAC VOVSIL S SADUF EPPOM FAFDULKA AOOIN Tris tries to follow it, to make something out of it— perhaps it is the language of the nation struck by disaster. XOVIPSAP POM KADAK KULKIJWOO MMOI SUYX ILJAF SECVUT After a moment, he decides this isn't a language at all. Whatever software provides the captioning has gone haywire; there is some glitch in the program that's turning the beautiful woman's words into gibberish—like a secret code generated by her voice.

Tris wants to keep watching the woman's green eyes and her flawed mouth and the stream of nonsense letters going past her, but the cloying melody of his cell phone chimes in his pocket. With some difficulty, he leans over and pulls the phone out, flipping it open all in one motion to see who's on the tiny screen before answering. Hopefully not Hal Pope. A number scrolls across, followed by an unexpected caller:

317-635-8800 MIDDLESBOROUGH PUBLIC LIBRARY

Tris recognizes the number immediately as the old exchange from his childhood: The area code is that of his home town, the medium-sized city with the circle at its heart that he tried to start drawing last night in his hotel room. And 635 is the exchange of the first phone number he ever stored in his fading memory—his own home number. Tris can still picture the number printed in that matter-of-fact fifties typeface on the celluloid circle in the middle of the orbit of numbers on the phone: MELROSE 2214. In those more poetic days, he lived within an exchange that the phone company named, and the entire broad expanse of his youth, the vast landscape where that singular someone named Tristan Holloway was shaped and formed, existed within the limits of the Melrose exchange, an area of some forty square blocks on the east side of the city.

He hesitates to answer the call. Why would the Middlesborough Public Library be calling? The sensation of having committed some long-ago transgression that's only now coming back to haunt him sends a flush of heat to his forehead. Overdue library books. Something he never returned when he was an irresponsible teenager, now years, decades overdue, the fine compounded to an astronomical amount.

The phone keeps chiming. As Tris is about to press TALK, the flight attendant places his hand firmly on Tris's shoulder.

"Excuse me, sir," he says, his voice dragging on the 'sir.' "All electronic devices must be turned off at this time. And all cell phones must remain off for the duration of the flight."

Tris glances at MIDDLESBOROUGH PUBLIC LIBRARY on the screen, then complies with the man. He flicks the button at the top of the phone and the screen shows him the word the phone's resident female voice is saying:

GOODBYE

Whoever it is, they will have to leave him a

message, and I'll get back to you as soon as possible." His voice, after all these years, hearing it again tight and faraway, sharp and distant. I hold the receiver closer to my face, his voice saying leave him a message and now I can't, I can't say a thing. The words won't come. I'm afraid to say anything, and I don't know what to say, I didn't practice it beforehand. I always thought I would just know, it would always be so simple and effortless between us, but that was long ago. It seems like someone else was talking on the other end of the line, a machine's voice answering. I have to put the phone down, lay it on the cradle and then he is

gone, outside maybe, perhaps they did go out to play, in the interval in which she laid her head down again and let herself be carried off by sleep. Perhaps they have wandered towards that murky retaining pond they call a lake in the name of the apartment complex: Lake Hamilton Village. She always reminds them not to go near the water, but children forget and do whatever pops into their heads. The vertical blinds cast long bars of shadow across the room, shrouding the couch in darkness. Late, she thinks. A whole day wasted. She sits up and folds her legs underneath her, the blanket still bunched around her knees and waist. Her throat is parched; she imagines it as a road dipping down a steep hill that has been paved with fresh tar.

Holly leaves the couch for the first time in hours. Her legs are stiff. The ball-shaped joint where her big toe articulates with her foot pops, as does her ankle, remnants of old horseback riding injuries. As she turns towards the kitchen, the room begins to spin, slowly, as if the apartment has been transformed into a carnival ride that has lurched into motion. The couch rotates towards the wall, which is rotating towards the cabinet that holds the TV, which rotates towards the front door, which rotates towards the blue armchair on the other side of the room, and she has to reach down and grab the moving arm of the couch to steady herself.

This is more than a hangover—there is something wrong. A dull presence has established itself at the base of her skull, a throbbing soreness that expands and contracts with each beat of her heart. She waits a moment, then puts her hands to the back of her head and rubs there, just behind the ears. She explores with her fingers the contours beneath the flesh of her scalp. There are two round lumps there—they should be

71

there—they are merely part of her skull where it dips in and sits on the top of her spine. But the places where her head hit the sink, twin centers of pain at the tender base of the skull, are sore to the touch. This is where the dull ache is coming from.

At least now she knows. For a while there, she thought she had given herself the worst hangover in the long history of her avid and ever-present drinking habit. Now she understands that it's simply the bruises from pounding her head on that damned sink. Now that she knows what the problem is, she can get on with her day and maybe do something with it, maybe take the kids to a movie and some dinner later on.

She enters the galley kitchen. Her stomach is a constricted knot of hunger, but maybe just a glass of water and back to the couch to lie down. She turns to the stove and sees a carton of ice cream sitting out on the counter. Ice cream would be good—cold, smooth, soothing to her throat. She opens the sweating lid of the carton and finds that the ice cream is melted, the whole thing reduced to a frothy white soup with chunks of chocolate floating in it. One of the girls must have left it out, probably Zoe.

Still . . . Holly opens the drawer and pulls out a spoon. Not just a teaspoon, a big serving spoon she can use to dip into the soup, making sure to catch the chocolate chips as she drags the surface. She slurps the warm juice into her mouth, catching the nuggets of chocolate with her tongue and working them back to her molars to chew. This makes her think of that stomach medicine her mother used to give her, Milk of Magnesia, but it does taste good, creamy. She drinks another spoonful and another, there is a large hole within her she must fill. It has always been there, as long as she can remember, and no matter what she does to fill it, it has never gone away. She dips the spoon into the liquid and as she's lifting it to her lips she remembers what Zoe said.

She was very mad at Grandpa Steve.

Holly puts the spoon down and goes to the living room, searching for the shard of porcelain, the fragment of pottery Zoe brought home. She looks on the low coffee table and on the floor in front of the television. She digs in the cracks between the cushions on the couch and she looks on the shelves of the cabinet where the kids keep their playthings. She goes to the girls' room, the bunk beds straight ahead and the desk they fight over when it's time to do their homework, the closet with the folding metal doors and the dresser where they keep their few clothes.

Of course. There it is, where Zoe keeps her special things, the rubber bouncy ball she found in the parking lot at the pizza place last week and the birthday card from her grandmother with the picture of the giraffe on it and the ribbon she won at field day for third place in the standing broad jump. There, in the nook between the headboard of the bottom bunk and the wall by the window.

Holly picks up the fragment of porcelain and holds it in both hands. It is like an artifact of an ancient civilization that carries with it through the centuries buried in dirt a significance that can only be grasped by an expert who has spent her entire life studying this culture. There is a hint, just a tip, of a light red blossom on the convex outside face. Otherwise, both the inside and out are milky smooth and white. Holly flips it over and turns it to see the shadows move across the hollowed out opposite face. And she knows; now she knows.

An idea comes to mind, more than an idea—a sudden urge. She wields the shard in one hand like a crude weapon, thumb on one edge, four fingers on the other with the sharp vertex of the curving wedge pointing down. And she brings the point gently to the exposed soft skin of her wrist, where the small hump of a blue vein crosses the outline of a tendon. She drags the tip lightly across her skin and a faint white mark appears. Yes, it will do it. She lifts it away for a moment, then brings it down again. This time, with a little more pressure, a tendril of blood appears. Keep going, keep ripping. The skin yields quite easily, like a tear in a cheap curtain, and a bubble of red comes out at the end when she stops. She closes her eyes and when she opens them again, she sees a vivid crimson stain on the tip of the white porcelain, the price she has to pay for letting it

happen
to me all the time, things like this happen, a missed phone call or the bus that just went past, but this time there was no problem, the man who asked me whether the 8 had gone by knew it hadn't, he was just drunk and trying to talk to me before he got around to asking for spare change for the fare. But it's not spare change anymore, it takes five quarters for a single oneway ride downtown if you don't have a pass. And sure enough, he got it from me, didn't he, a dollar bill and a quarter. He sits down first and I go to the back past some young black men talking about

jobs they can get at Wilder Mission. I've seen them before, they know me. They would stop the drunk before he did anything to hurt me, and anyway I've seen worse on the bus coming home, men who look like they'd just as soon knife you as spit in your eye. Mother used to bring us downtown to shop on Saturday afternoons like this, holding our hands tight like holding those girls' hands going across the street, the clock above the department store jutting from the corner of the building, green, ornate and famous. We always said, "Meet me under the clock." Now it tells the wrong time, frozen at nine twenty seven. The day Louise told them, you were supposed to meet me under the clock, but you never

came to the back room first, the voice of her youngest extending through the mist of unconsciousness to bring her back from wherever it was she was headed, a depth of submerged underwater feeling, a place so cold she felt as if she were lying face down and naked in a hard empty bathtub with all the lights on, her face smashed against the tub, and when she first heard Zoe's voice scream, all she wanted to do was ask Zoe to bring her a blanket. If someone would just bring her a blanket, she could keep lying here and drift back into the depths of wherever she was headed, dim dark circles opening one after the other, wider and wider to float down into. But Zoe screamed again, and this time Holly felt someone grab her arm, a child's feverish hand, the warmth of it making Holly's eyes open.

A vast landscape of light beige bumps extends in all directions with a large hand—her own hand, it must be—directly in front of her. In the far distance she can see one leg of the bunk bed and the beige bumps clarify themselves into the nap of the wall-to-wall carpet they have in this apartment. They will have to replace it. Holly sees that there will be a terrible stain, right next to the girls' beds, a reminder to them all each night when she tucks them in to sleep. The beige bumps in the immediate foreground near her wrist are coated with a slick expanse of crimson liquid.

Now another voice joins Zoe's screaming. High, tight, pierced with shrillness.

"Get *away* from her, you idiot." Jenny, always bossing.

"What happened?" Zoe asks, her voice shaken between the intake of breath and a sob.

"Look, that broken piece you brought back. It must have cut her."

Holly's eyes close, before she can lift her head to answer. Maybe better to go now, back to those circles expanding wider and wider, deep as they were into a darkness that grows and grows.

"We gotta call 9-1-1."

"No," Jenny's voice says, firmly, taking charge. "Call Tom. I'll call him. He'll be here faster."

Tom, oh no not Tom. Her eyes open but her mouth doesn't, even though she wants to speak. Cold. A shudder of draining bloodlessness overtakes her body. Don't call Tom, she wants to say. She doesn't want him to see her this way, doesn't want to see him at all. Don't call him ever again, why should I have expected anything to come of this escapade, this outrageous lie I've been living now for years upon years, this semblance of him built up inside me, a beckoning bronze statue of an ancient hero with his arm thrust out, he calls to me across the years, his voice, his smile. It can't be the same, but it is ever the same inside me. It lives and grows and still I want him to my self inside. I am still me, and he is still Tris, and we are still together. We want each other just the same, we never quarreled, never parted, and even then it wasn't really a quarrel but a grand misunderstanding. There was no reason why we should not have been together, though the others saw it differently, and he let himself be swayed by them, by my father and Louise, her petty jealousies always wedging herself between us, though she never wanted him and never could. She couldn't bear to see us happy, and look at her now, her whole side of the family a wreck. What did they matter, none of them mattered as much to me as Tris, I see him now as if he is a portrait forever painted inside my head, his dark hair gleaming and his silver blue eyes glancing at me when they weren't supposed to, and that portrait of him has never left, ingrained within a part of me that shall never

die or end up

here. A door slams in the corridor beyond the curtain that partially conceals the bed Holly is lying in. These people are noisy. Hospitals are supposed to be quiet places. When she was a young child and lived in an apartment in the city, the large general hospital serving the indigent of Middlesborough was only a few blocks away, and each night the mournful wailing of the

77

ambulance sirens making their desperate runs would wake her and frighten her, as if the sirens were coming to take her. Yet there was a sign at the end of her street admonishing those who drove past:

HOSPITAL

QUIET

She closes her eyes again and slumps her head back. A slow, steady ticking noise dribbles down from directly above her, a machine measuring something, marking time or perhaps the beating of her heart. Make it stop, she thinks. If this ticking is me, then please make it stop.

"Holly," a voice says, from the other side of the bed. "You're awake." Waiting and hoping for her to rise. That would be Tom, he never could leave well enough alone. They must have called him. The girls, of course they did. Jenny always wanting her to see Tom, likes him more than she does, sees him as the father she never has had, but might. Sweet, suffocating Tom.

Always trying too hard, he will never leave her alone. And now here he is, back again.

"Holly, it's me," he says, as if she doesn't know. "Tom."

His voice is soothing soft, like a pillow someone is smothering her with. She keeps her eyes closed and pretends to be sleeping still. A great weariness adheres to the pressure she feels from Tom's voice, the subtle expectation of his wanting her to be something more than she ever will be. And beyond this weariness is the realization that the cool dark hole she had been drifting into has vanished.

Tom is silent now, always good, letting her rest. But his eyes are still on her, she knows. He is watching her and, what she cannot bear, adoring her in his eager way, like a parent who has come to check on a slumbering child. During the few weeks they were seeing each other earlier in the summer, he would appear in the dim vestibule of her apartment building clutching some small gift he had brought her—roses from a roadside stand or a CD he wanted her to have of one of his favorite bands. And this would set the tone for the evening, starting them off out of balance, him giving more than she could—or would; setting up a scaffolding of external pressure that made the conversation feel forced and tense. One thing about Tom: he has money. And that added to the imbalance.

He would take her to the best restaurants—not trendy places like Midtown Grill, but really upscale fine-dining restaurants where she felt totally out of her depth. These were the big downtown places where he and the other lawyers and power brokers from the Statehouse did their deals, where they gave her too many forks to keep track of and her clothes were never quite dressy enough. These restaurants were always too quiet—she felt as if the waiters were watching her and listening in on what she had to say. And afterwards he would take her to a concert or sporting event with front row seats and they never had a bad time, she always at the end of the night had to admit she enjoyed it, but still there was the sense of owing him something, of a debt to be paid, and, finally, what made her nearly always turn him away with little more than a kiss: the off-putting feeling that he was simply trying too hard.

Holly doesn't want to open her eyes, but the lids flutter and white light pours in. The eyelids flicker again and remain open.

Tom looks at her and smiles. Then, always trying to anticipate her needs, he pours water into a styrofoam cup and offers it to her.

She takes it and drinks, feeling the liquid slip into her like another one of Tom's unrequited gifts, getting his grip on her again. She closes her eyes and tries to drift into those expanding, dark circles that were pulling her down, but Tom is in her head again. She rejected him so cruelly a few weeks ago that she believed he would never come back, in spite of Jenny asking after him. The girl must have sensed in Tom what repelled Holly: his stability, his bland goodness, his caring responsibility. Even after Holly broke off their brief and never fully consummated relationship, she has had the sense that he has been lurking out there, waiting for something like this to happen, a chance for him to swoop in and prove his worth to her and the girls.

Another person has entered the room, a nurse taking notes concerning the machine above her head, writing down numbers and data Holly's body has generated. The nurse's hair is bleached blond and bedraggled, hanging in limp loose strands she has to keep tossing back from her eyes as she checks the bag of fluid suspended from a pole and connected to Holly's forearm by a plastic tube. She could use a good cut, more of her natural color. The blond doesn't go with her skin; it makes her face look pasty and white. She goes about her business intently, as if Holly isn't lying half naked on the bed watching what she does. Tom watches her too, his lawyer's mind cataloging the facts on this case, taking its own notes.

Abruptly, the nurse looks up at Tom, never catching Holly's eye, and makes an announcement.

"The doctor will be in to see you." But she doesn't say when. She turns on her heels and slouches out of the room.

Tom has drafted a critique of her performance. Lining up pieces of evidence that could be used in a case. "She didn't check your wound. Are the bandages comfortable?"

Holly has been afraid to look. She doesn't want to think of what she did to herself as a wound, an injury that must heal. It was more of a pathway, an opening that would take her someplace else. Away from this. A wrap of tight gauze clings to the place where the cut was made, a bracelet of white cloth with a thick pad turned brown as rust where the blood once flowed.

"It's fine," she says, not giving him the satisfaction of having something to lobby for with the nurse or the doctor. Tom. Standing there watching her beyond the bars at the side of the bed as if she holds something precious within her. He would tell her how beautiful she was, trying always to find just the right word to give her, as if he were holding up a mirror to her face, her body, trying to make them look better than they really were. Despite all his efforts, it's a case he could never win. She wanted to tell him that holding her up on a pedestal was the wrong approach. She needed someone to debase her, to confirm her worst notions of her self, someone who would slam her head into a porcelain basin and break her. Tom circles around to the other side of the bed and inspects the bag of fluid dripping into her, reading the small blue print as if he might deduce something about her treatment from it. Though it's a Saturday, he looks as if he could have come straight from a business meeting. His button-down blue dress shirt puffing out from the waist where it is tucked into khaki pants with pleats that make his hips look wide and womanly. His cell phone strapped onto his belt to the right of his fly, ready for action, like a stubby metallic prick. She remembers telling him one night on a date that wearing the phone on his belt made him look ridiculous and insecure, but he refused to remove it, an attachment he couldn't do without.

"I came as soon as Jenny called. I hope you don't mind."

Don't apologize, she thinks, looking at the pads of flesh that extend his cheeks beyond the wire rims of his glasses and break the smooth line of his jaw. It makes her want to swat him aside. The one man who should have apologized to her never did.

"You probably saved my life," she says, keeping her voice flat, not giving him anything to latch onto. "Not that it matters."

"What do you mean by that?" He comes closer now. He has earned the right to lean over the bars on the bed and put his chubby face near. "This cut . . . " He pauses and motions towards her arm, letting his gesture express a meaning he won't say. "The girls said it was an accident."

She will not give him the satisfaction of knowing what this is about. He shouldn't be here injecting himself into her life again.

"Of course it was. I was looking at a piece of broken pottery Zoe brought back from the sitter and it cut me."

His eyes try to lock onto hers, try to pin her down. Behind the thick lenses the brown irises are enlarged, the pupils distended.

"That's an unusual place to have something just cut you…"

"Don't interrogate me, Tom. If you want to start that shit, you can leave."

She has never had any problem being a bitch. There has always been the need to deflect people away from her when they get too close. Especially someone like Tom who wants to tie her down. She imagines him strapping her arms and legs to this hospital bed like they do to the prisoners or crazy people who are sick. She has to go on the offensive with him.

"Where are the girls?"

"They got tired of waiting. Hospitals are boring places. I had the TV on for them, but for some reason you can only get three channels, so I suggested they go to the gift shop and get a snack." He backs off, standing more upright beside the bed again. "They are very concerned about their mother. Zoe in particular. She's blaming herself for this."

They must still be in the emergency ward, not a real hospital room, for taped to the wall behind Tom's big head is a poster that shows the back of a human torso with the skin removed to reveal the deftly woven baskets of muscle that knit the body together. The corners of the poster are torn where it had been taped to a different wall previously. Someone put it up here as a kind of grim decoration. There are cutaways revealing the more interior bony structures. And beside the full torso of muscle and bone, there is a side view of the notched bones of the spine, interlocking like a chain, appearing in its elongated sinuous curve as nothing so much as the skeleton of a snake. Beneath it, the flat girdle of the bones of the pelvis are displayed, which makes Holly think for some reason with its spreading wings of a dried-out cow's skull. The poster is called THE AMAZING BACK. Something a doctor can use to point out what's wrong with you. Seeing these elaborate structures that conspire to give us form and function makes Holly curl up deeper within the pain at the back of her head, sink into her animal self. Closing her eyes again, she has a dim understanding that these mechanisms of flesh and bone must all work together perfectly to keep us alive.

Her mind forms a question that will divert him.

"How is your work going?" She knows that if she gets him started on this, he cannot help but talk about it.

"Oh, you know. Always the same partisan crap at the Statehouse. I've been working for eighteen months on the contracts for the new prison they want to build in Henderson, and it keeps getting stalled in committee. But they need it. The one they have now is filled to overflowing. Thirty-six percent above the legally allowable capacity, and the feds are taking away funding because of it. Every few weeks it seems some rapist or murderer they let out early to make room has killed someone again." He starts pacing the floor as he talks about it. "It's a growth industry, building prisons." He looks at her and shrugs his beefy shoulders. "What do I care? Either way, I get paid."

Yes, he does get paid, very well. The bald fact of his money has always hung there between them, like his stubby cell phone, an electromagnetic device that can both repel and attract. Tom's thoughts have been directed into the orbit of his work for the moment, and in his distraction he falls into the old habits of his technical curiosity, stepping carefully around to the other side of the bed to scrutinize the elaborate device that is recording the stream of data being produced by Holly's body. He rests his hand on the bar at the side of Holly's bed, and Holly observes it with the same technical dispassion. A curled star, hairless and well manicured, accustomed to working with papers and documents. Unbidden, the hand that turned the pages in that red book enters her head. Hands can do so many things, for better and for worse. She rolls her eyes away and sees the rippling mountains of Tom's shirt, a landscape bulging with contours that shift and distort as he reaches up to touch the display screen above her head. His body was never unattractive to her; that was not the reason she never gave herself to him. All bodies have their own attractions. She often wondered what it would be like to have sex with him, a body padded and upholstered with flesh like a comfortable old couch. There is a curiosity about everyone new that is in fact perhaps the chief source of her seeking, the reason she is afraid of being tied down to a single man. The shock of having a new body exposed to her, like the raw, glossy photos on the pages of that book—the mind thrilled by a fresh set of sensations. Hard to imagine that Tom's heavy broad back is underwoven with the same basket of muscles depicted on the poster taped to the wall, but even the most decrepit human bodies are a miracle in their finely tuned functioning, a treasure, as the poster baldly states: Amazing.

Another door slams in the corridor beyond. There is a sense of hurry here—these patients must be seen and cured and moved along. Another batch of injured and ill will be coming in soon.

"Tom," she says, trying his name again, feeling it come out awkward and clipped. "I wanted to thank you. For coming when the girls called."

He doesn't turn around immediately—he senses an opening, what he has been waiting for. Then, the full force of his brown eyes is upon her.

"It was nothing. Jenny said I make a pretty good ambulance driver. We laid you in the back seat and Jenny crouched down in the floor well and watched over you, and I kept Zoe in front with me. She seemed to be the most upset by it." He tries to soften. "They loved it when I laid on the horn, honking all the way through the red lights." And then, to let her know he wasn't taking unnecessary risks with the girls in the car. "You were bleeding pretty bad. Blood everywhere."

"In your nice car? My God, it must be ruined."

"Don't worry, I can take it to the dealer to be cleaned. And if not, it's about time for a new one anyway. I'm thinking more along the lines of a Range Rover, something a little more rugged. I don't like the styling of the new Beamers."

The squeak of many sneakers on the floor announces the girls to them. Zoe comes first, rushing her round face close to the metal bar that separates the realm of the bed from the rest of the room.

"Mommy!" she cries, her curly hair wavering, her cheeks red with the heat of conflicting emotions. She presses up on her tippy-toes to get her face over the bar, and Holly leans over to meet her there, accepting the energetic kiss she plants near the corner of her mouth. When the face is withdrawn, Holly can see that it is still draped with a cloud of fear as she furtively glances down the bedrail towards the bandage that encircles her mother's wrist.

"It's okay sweet," Holly says. She lifts the arm above the railing to show her that the arm is still usable, still functioning in spite of the wound. "Just a silly cut. They patched me up and I'm going to be fine." Jenny has been observing from afar, hanging back by the wall where the poster of the skinned torso maintains its sentinel station. And despite Holly's tepid demonstration, she sees that Zoe's face is still clouded by fear or guilt—probably both. Something more is needed.

"Zoe, this isn't your fault. I was looking for that piece of pottery and when I found it I was clumsy. You know how clumsy I can be . . . " Holly sends a smile with these words, trying to lift her girls out of the gloom she has created. Of course she should not leave them. That cool dark place that was calling her, with her girls standing near it seems a fragment of a dream that has settled into a night gone by. "Remember the time I sliced my finger open cutting the apple? That was an accident too." And she has to thank Jenny, who has been growing more distant every day, her budding young teenager.

"It was scary, Mom," Zoe says with a bit of relief in her voice now that the guilt has been lifted away from her. "All the blood . . . " Her voice trails off, burnished with the images that have been seared into her. Somehow, Holly thinks, she will have to make amends. Over time, she will have to make it up to them.

"You did the right thing, calling Tom. He tells me he's a very good ambulance driver."

"You should have seen us." The excitement of this afternoon has been more of an adventure to Jenny, like the crimes and family disputes she sees on reality TV shows suddenly come to life in her own bedroom. "Weaving in and out of the cars, running red lights. It was like one of those police chases on Most Extreme Videos." Then, ashamed of her own excitement, she qualifies her description. "We were afraid we wouldn't get you here in time."

Tom seeks to make his mark in all this, to cement his new-found status within this truncated family of women.

"Jenny was great. So calm. She knew exactly what to do. Applying pressure on the cut, elevating the arm." He approaches the girl and swings his arm around her, drawing her near. But instead of returning the embrace as Holly has seen her do many times before, her daughter tenses and pulls away, the muscles of her back taut and rigid, banded across the shoulder blades by the tight T-shirt she wears, her body transformed from that of an innocent girl into a collection of parts that will be used by others over the years to come for their pleasure and gratification, nothing more than a collection of

parts of me scattered all over this place, in the powder room we'd go to freshen up, standing before the mirror, rouging our cheeks and lining our eyes, making ourselves up, watchful of the other faces captured in the mirror. Who was seeing whom, that was the fluttery talk in that room, sound of voices bouncing off the tiles, feathery breath above powdered bosoms displayed like fruit the boys could only see, not touch. In the lobby smoking cigarettes, in the balconies hanging above the mezzanine, parts of me in the coffee shop in the corridors that went to the hotel. We ran when they brought us here as children, it was a castle climbing the grand staircase, leaning over the railing, watching the people mill around below. The gentle sound of the little gong struck with a padded mallet, three parts of me, three tones, calmly calling the audience back from intermission.

Elmer in his suspenders looking tall and grand, Tris slim and smiling, dark hair, eyes celluloid blue like a movie screen in the moment before it's lit up with a film. Louise fawning, gaping, her dress full of flowers on her pallid body, breasts already jutting out, you couldn't help but look. Parts of me scattered all over this place, the seats the same seats, plush velveteen, purple cushions swaying back. We rode the number 8 streetcar here by ourselves, on Saturdays just like this one, they'd never let kids do that now, never see them in one piece again. Tris and Elmer cracking peanut shells during the film, stifling a laugh. Louise aloof, above it all with her breasts heaving a sigh and glancing, her eyes disdainful. I could feel you, knew you were there, we were mixed together like the particles of light and dust from the broad beam of the projector dancing narrow at the top and then ever wider, advancing over the gaping pit of the mezzanine seats, broadening and dancing with dust until it filled the screen together.

They want us to come now for dinner in the grand ballroom above the theater, parts of me scattered here too. Dances they had, summer cotillions, proms in the spring, we never went to one together, never went but I saw you with others, felt you across the room, glancing, saying hello like we knew, we always had someone else between us. Even with Louise gone and off to college, first college girl in the family, her forehead high as her bosom, and now look at her. I never did it—I never let them, always saving myself for Tris, always keeping myself for him.

What if I saw him tonight—too many people, too many years gone by, could it ever be the same? People floating in the room like dust in the light, a mock Spanish village with a dome of high stars, blue evening tending to dusk, surrounding the same dance floor we used to use. They would never think to build such a lovely thing now, never spend the money to create something as lovely as this, and now they want to tear it down, destroy it. Pieces of me, parts of me they will destroy, tearing it down in three days. In three days it will be all gone, parts of me scattered all over the place.

Scanning the vast room, I cannot see his face, any face that means anything to me, all sallow and drawn, all withered and covered with splotches, so I am not the only one who has aged. What would he look like? All of us worse for wear, even this beautiful old building is, but better off than most of us. It still has a grandeur, that grandeur they used to build into things. Can it really be fifty years since the proms, the cotillions, the Saturday nickel movie shows, smoke wafting up in the lobby. There's Margaret, yes Margaret Borden, her family ran the five and dime on Jefferson just down the way.

"Margaret Borden, is that you?"

"No, not Borden any more." Smiling, eyes lifting up to see who I might be. "My name is Lentz, has been now for forty-seven years. Why, Amelia Geist, dear Lord, I remember you. How have you been? It's so good to see you. My word, Burt, it's Amelia Geist, come and say hello."

He offers his hand, shaking mine and then he takes it up to his mouth and kisses it. Burt Lentz, a grade or two higher than us, maybe Louise's age.

"Yes, of course," he says. "I remember the Geists. How could I forget, Louise was in my class.

"Yes," Margaret says, jealous of not so much me as the memory of Louise. Thank God she won't be here. "Yes, I remember Louise."

"She was a stunner," he says. "A beauty. All the boys wanted to date her. So haughty though, and aloof. She was unattainable. My God, Louise Geist, whatever happened to her? Last I heard, she was off to college. Going to be an English professor someday, or a writer." I want to tell them the memory of her is better than the truth, want to bring her down a peg finally, bring her down in the eyes of others. But no, it wouldn't be right. Let them think what they will. That memory, that piece of her should still live at least in this building, this grand building.

"She's doing very well. Married and living in the beautiful hills outside of Bremerton, a writer."

"We always thought she would be a writer."

"Yes," I say, lying. I cannot bear to see this piece of her rent asunder. "Yes, she has been married," not true, "married these many years and living happily, writing for magazines and journals."

"How about you, Amelia? So good to see you. This place is still so wonderful." Margaret smiling now that the subject has moved on from Louise. "We came all the way from Florida for this. Wouldn't miss it for the world—such wonderful memories. What a shame they have to tear it down."

Burt hooks his arm in Margaret's and leads us to a table, playing the role of the stern, practical man. "Yes," he says, "but it's all for the better. This real estate is too valuable to have it taken up by an old theater nobody uses any more and an old folks home. They can put an office building here and generate a whole future revenue stream of rents. Now this place is generating nothing in terms of income or taxes for the city."

I want to tell him how wrong he is. There are vacant buildings three blocks from here, why can't they tear those down instead? But no, hold your lip Amelia, always holding your lip, always keeping things nice for others, deferring, letting them go about their business, their lives. Margaret wants to tell me about her life. She asked but never bothered to listen to mine.

"Seven grandchildren," she says, bragging, a magical number. "We have them down to see us each year, as long as they keep coming. Retired in Ninety-three, fourteen years ago. Burt sold the business, and we moved where it's warm." She sees that my hands are empty except for the signet ring Karl left me, not a thing on my left hand. She places her hand on the linen tablecloth where I can't help but see it, showing me what her life has been like, her hands fat like two loaves of bread burnished with spots, showing me the sun her skin has endured, showing me the ring embedded in the fat of her fourth finger, buried in flesh together with this man. Where are you Tris, where

have you been? I've been frantic here."

"What do you mean?" he says, resting the portfolio on top of the suitcase with the roller wheels, setting his things down, glad to be home. "I've been working. I was in Wichita, at a convention."

"I called several times and you didn't answer the phone." She lays the paint brush on the rim of the can and bats a loose strand of hair away from her eyes. "I've been trying to reach you. I didn't have any idea when you were getting back, and we have the contractors coming over today to tear out the deck. As a matter of fact, they're here now."

She looks thinner than when he left; the whole house looks more sparse. Things have changed. Laura has been, as she put it, frantic, charging around the house getting rid of things, de-cluttering, neutralizing, preparing the house to put it on the market. Tris isn't quite sure what the rush is, why all of a sudden there is such a pressing need to sell this place he has grown comfortable in over twenty-seven years, but it must have something to do with the surge of manic energy that has overtaken her in the past six months. It's as if there is a new, strange woman in the house living with him, a thinner, harder, colder version of the woman he used to know, bent on survival at all costs. Bound and determined to get out of this place and move on, whether he decides to join her or not.

As Tris walks across the kitchen floor to empty his pockets of keys, wallet, cell phone, pen, and loose change, he hears a funny echo. The precise clump of his shoes on the wood is louder, more pronounced than he recalls. And then he realizes that it is because all the knick-knacks that used to be on the counter and breakfast table are gone. The framed photographs of the children and grandchildren have disappeared, the heavy glass candlesticks, the vase that once held fresh-cut flowers from the garden, the basket that contained a stack of paper napkins, the wooden bowl for fresh fruit, the drift of three-day-old newspapers and last week's magazines and unpaid bills: all gone. Even the small metal box where he flings the loose change from his pockets when he arrives home is gone. Decluttered. He is left holding a fistful of quarters, nickels, and dimes, with nowhere to put them except back in his pocket.

She probably cashed in all those old coins for bills— probably twenty or thirty dollars worth sitting there, accumulating—and threw away the box. That's what this is all about, when he gets right down to it: Cashing in. For nearly forty-three years this woman has been relying on him to feed her, clothe her, support her children, but now that time is nearly finished, and she is busy declaring her freedom from him. Wiping away all the accumulated clutter that his hard work bought. His useful life as breadwinner, sole supporter, will be over in a few short weeks. The equity in this house built up over the years, another kind of accumulation, will soon become her chief source of income, and his status has been downgraded accordingly.

"Why are you painting the kitchen brown?" The place has smelled like wet paint for weeks. First the guest bedrooms where the kids used to sleep, then the downstairs bath and the living room, now this. All the wallpaper gone. All the bright cheerful colors that made the house feel like an Italian villa: gone. And in their place gallons of white or beige paint, ugly no-colors that make the house feel empty and bare, like another hotel room he is visiting.

"It's not brown, it's taupe."

"Oh, taupe." He opens an empty drawer to the left of the sink where a tangled jumble of extension cords, measuring tape, glue sticks, hammers, pliers, screw drivers, batteries, and non-functional flashlights used to live, fishes the coins out of his pocket and drops them in. "Never heard of it."

"Cindy says we have to neutralize as much as possible to get the maximum value out of the house." She takes another swipe at the wall with her paint brush, keeping her back to him while she talks. "Neutralize and declutter. People don't want to see a house that looks like the current owners are living there. They want everything to be immaculate, to look like they could move right in without a trace of the former owners. People want to be able to flip the house in a year or two. They don't plan on staying in one place forever like we did."

This comes as a form of accusation: They could have made more money if he had been clever enough to sell their house and move to a new place every few years. Ever since her pal Cindy got her real estate license in the spring, Laura has been dispensing Cindy's found wisdom about housing prices in the Bay Area and whether or not the overheated market is a bubble that's about to burst. Tris feels as if he is listening to a tape recording of Cindy after she's had two or three Margueritas, all these newfound and strongly held opinions coming out of Laura's mouth about chemicals in the food she eats, zoning ordinances, and who should be elected to the local school board.

"Well, the current owner would like something for dinner. I'm starving. They never feed you on these flights anymore. They actually had the gall to walk up and down the aisle offering a box with a stale sandwich and a bag of pretzels for five dollars."

Laura twists her head around to see if he is serious about eating, then returns to her painting. Her iron red hair drapes the crew-neck collar of her t-shirt, but even her hair, which Tris has prized as his wife's most resonant feature, seems somehow drained of color, more filaments of silver in it than ever before.

"It's too early for dinner," she says, her wrist avidly spreading taupe across the wall. "I had no idea when you would get here. Or even *if* you would get here." The way she says this implies that he has forfeited any chance of dinner tonight. "I haven't even started thinking about dinner yet."

"It's not too early where I came from. It's late for me."

"You need to get out there with those guys, the contractors. I don't trust them."

"And why is that?"

"It's a father and son. Tell me how many fathers and sons can work together without getting mad at each other and screwing something up."

"That's just you, speaking from your own experience. With our own son."

"No, there's something about his eyes, the son. I don't like the way he looked around the house, like he was casing the place to see what we have to steal."

"You're getting paranoid. Besides, what can they screw up? They're just tearing out the deck."

"I have good reason to be paranoid, with all these strange men tromping in and out of the house." She puts down the paint brush and turns to look at him. The face he sees is a familiar face, a worn out face. She's been working herself too hard. He takes a step towards her, anticipating that she may finally want to embrace him, to welcome him home, but she brushes past to look out the window towards the pool in back of the house. "I can't even see what they're doing. I want you to go out there and see what's going on."

He places his hand on the shoulder of her paint-spackled shirt and finds it to be hard, rigid, like the shoulder of a teenage boy. Despite his touch, she does not turn to him, and he doesn't dare go any further. He removes his hand and steps away.

Tris exits the decluttered house through the sliding glass door at the back of the sunken family room. The pebbled concrete of the pool deck bounces hot sheets of afternoon sun into his face as he circles towards the side of the house. A shimmer of wavering green light hugs the rounded cornices of the pool wall, making him pause for a moment. The water is supple, dense, a body at rest breathing with a rhythm of its own. There is a barely perceptible skin of dust or dirt floating on the water, a film of disuse that may be fallen ash from brush fires in the hills or merely the residue of the ever-present smog. At the shallow end, a collection of brittle cypress leaves and a deflating rubber raft hover near the intake of the water filter. The floor of the liver-shaped pool tilts down at a steep angle to the drain at the bottom of the deep end, which is darkened by the distended shadow of the diving board. The children who grew up in this house and their children too when they came to visit once loved to fling themselves off this flexible plank into the water, shouting slogans from action hero movies or cartoons they had seen, pretending to imitate famous people or inanimate objects.

As each generation grew older, the fascination of the board faded away, and Tris considers now whether any of them will ever disturb the still water of the pool again. A vibration stirs the skin of dust on the water, a momentary breeze that makes the deep end look cool and inviting. Would he sink or float? What makes a twenty-story ocean liner float on top of the deep sea while a helpless human form plunges to the bottom of a pool? The wavering drain at the bottom stares up at him, menacing. A faint whiff of chlorine turns him away.

From around the corner of the house he hears voices, the contractors busy with their work. This section of his small lot has always felt barren and forlorn. Here, the spiny shrubs are untended and overgrown, and a faint trembling of apprehension lifts in his stomach as he turns into the irregular side yard where the cedar deck is being hacked into pieces.

Perhaps Laura is right to be concerned about the contractors and day laborers that have been parading through the house lately. Any one of these men could overpower her, alone in the house, pin her down on one of the tarps they throw on the floor and rape her. Perhaps one of these men will steal something from him—credit cards, jewelry, important papers. Yet, as with most of the world's catastrophes, it seems like a horror that could only afflict someone else.

Two men in loose jeans and t-shirts are bent over their work, their arms jerking as they pry up boards near the wrought-iron railing at the far side of the deck. Tris watches them for a moment, wondering what it would be like to make a living with his hands instead of his wits, giving an honest day's work with sweat and tired muscles instead of always talking to people, persuading, convincing, and apologizing to them. One of the men, the shorter one, round with a belly that folds upon itself as he bends to his task, grunts and calls to his partner, the one who must be his son. The broad cedar deck, once stained a vivid red, has faded to a dead brown laced with an emerald layer of moss that has creeped over it during years of neglect. In the shadow of the house, the air smells of dried pine needles.

The younger man says something in Spanish, his words coming out mumbled and soft. The older laborer looks up and sniffs, like a dog that hears a noise in the distance too high-pitched for humans. Then he produces a laugh, a quick stifled snort that indicates he is aware of Tris's presence. He hoists a pickaxe high above his head, then wrenches his shoulders to slam it down into the mid-section of a cedar board at his feet. The wood snaps and buckles in two. Ragged splinters tear apart from each broken end of the board. For a brief moment, the two segments still hang together by the connective tissue of several fibers that have refused to yield. Then, with a sudden explosion of force that startles Tris, the younger man hurls the heavy head of a sledgehammer into the crease where the two parts of the board are joined. As the black bulk of the hammer crashes into the wood, Tris fears for an instant that it will smash the feet of the father, so close by. But these two are accustomed to wreaking their havoc together. The blow delivered by the son is followed in quick succession by the blunt end of the father's awl digging into the shattered wood and lifting it with a dry creaking crack apart and away from the body of the other boards.

Tris nods at the men, hoping they will acknowledge his presence, but they drive on with their plangent work, hands grasping, arms churning, brows lathered with sweat. They have no time for pleasantries with him. The sun is gathering itself to the far hills beyond the broad freeways and shopping malls, the

100

shadows of the pine arbors are growing longer. With a final sudden crack, a great section of board flies free from the rest, skidding across the planks, revealing the moist hidden dirt that lies beneath. Tris inches closer as they snatch loose another section of rotting wood. The earth beneath these boards has been covered for years, fallow and rich, desecrated only by a few stray scraps of litter that have blown in from the open end by the firepit, a damp plastic grocery bag, a paper coffee cup, a fast food hamburger wrapper.

The younger worker, the son, kicks one of the rotten boards they have knocked loose with his boot, kicks it aside as if he is angry at it, a piece of debris that stands between him and the end of the day, where dinner and a six pack of beer await. In the rich earth newly exposed, Tris sees something move. He steps closer to get a better look. Yes, there, squirming into the dirt to escape whatever it was that came crashing down upon them, tiny white globules, like burrowing sacs of milk, brown and white larvae-like creatures tunneling into the muck. To think of this swarm of mindless life, carrying on its activities hidden beneath their feet, digging, reproducing; the sight of them pinches his lips together in disgust. With his eyes calm and intense, the son steps into the hole and stomps the solid tread of his boot onto the writhing bugs. Several are smashed instantly, popping open to emit an oozing milky fluid. Others squirm away quickly, the bulbous tail ends of their abdomens disappearing into the earth.

"What are they?" Tris asks, shielding his mouth with his hand.

"*Comején,*" the older man says, glancing at the wall of the house.

"What?" Tris wonders if either of them speaks any English. "*No comprende.*"

The son digs his heel in, squashing a few of the stragglers, intent on his task. Thankful for this break, the father lays the pickaxe down on the deck.

"*Termitas,*" he says, pronouncing the word slowly, for Tris's benefit. The son heaves the sledgehammer into the boards once more, cracking loose another chunk of rotten wood, exposing another hive of the industrious insects. Tris's mind flicks towards the house, imagining the teeming hidden life that could be eating away at the foundations. The son kicks the wood he has just broken, knocking it vaguely in the direction of the pile of debris he is creating, but mostly just knocking it away

from

here as soon as we could. We love the Florida lifestyle." She goes on telling, aggrandizing all of it as if the things we do each day, eating, sleeping, watching TV and the rest are any better in a different place because the weather is warmer or the sun is shining instead of the rain or there is an ocean down the street instead of a cornfield. "Fourteen years ago, the first night on Sanibel, we couldn't believe we were there, like a different world, but it was so cold that night, record cold they said. It nearly snowed, and it was like we brought the winter down with us."

Burt laughing, his hand goes to fork a piece of lettuce into his mouth. "The guys at the club I was playing with the next day gave me so much grief about it. We nearly froze our . . . well, I won't say it. I was so thrilled to be playing golf in January, I had nothing but a polo shirt on, and they said 'Burt you old snow-bird, you brought this damn cold with you.'"

Margaret, we never did call her Maggie, she wouldn't deign to be called it even back in grade school, always Margaret, reaches for the butter, reaches across and spreads it as if she is anointing someone's foot. Words coming out even as she lifts the bread to eat. "It never has been that cold again. Every winter since is just like May or June up here."

"That's right," he says. "You maybe get four or five months a year of decent weather here, maybe four, but we live for winter. Just the right coolness in the morning, breeze off the gulf. Sweater weather, we call it. And then sixty-five and sunny by noon."

Bread delicious with butter, iced tea ice crackling in the glass with lemon and lots of sugar, and chicken with a sauce, asparagus and little slivers of potato garnished with flecks of green, like eating a coin that melts in your mouth. I haven't had a meal like this in a very long time, maybe since Elmer's funeral. But he is going on again. "Where's the wine?" He practically shouts it across the room. Some of the others sitting across the table turn to look. "You'd think they could at least manage to get a decent bottle of wine on the table."

"Burt, it's okay. You can't expect a place like this, practically falling down of its own weight, to do any better."

"Well hell, if they won't feed us properly they should at least give us something to drink." The others are looking now. He knows he's making a scene. "I do believe there is a jigaboo liquor store that operates not two blocks from here up Illinois Street. I can go and buy us a good bottle of scotch if you like."

"No darling, you should probably take a . . . "

"I need a good stiff one. Finally got out of this two-bit hick town, and now I remember why I left."

"Oh come Burt, we can be cordial. The meal is not the reason we are here. We're here to see all these wonderful people we grew up with, Amelia, and can you believe we saw Jonesy McCutcheon by the bandstand?" He is desecrating this place, a great vibration welling up. These rafters have withstood more than this spattering of words though, have seen the span of two centuries.

"Hey Mele," he calls me that now, as if we're old friends. "Whatever happened to Tris Holloway? Do you ever see him?" His face smiling, teeth jutting out like a wall of bone draped with flesh, like he knows something.

"Yes," she says. "Tris Holloway. Dear lord, I haven't thought about old Tris in all these years. He was such a happy-go-lucky kind of guy. Whatever happened to Tris?"

"I really don't know. I haven't seen him in many years myself."

"Oh really?" he says, latching on to something. Pleased to have found something to prod me with, his teeth a wall of bone. "I thought the two of you were an item back when. Always over at Haag's together at the soda fountain. I remember you Geists traveled in a pack, you and Elmer and Tris and Louise.

"Yes," she says, smiling too, joining in this remembrance, "but Tris wasn't really a Geist, he was a Holloway. Burt, you know that."

"Oh yes," his teeth clamping together on the words like something he bit off and chewed. "But didn't he seem like a Geist? He and Elmer were always out smoking in the back of the gym along that wall where the boiler room was." What to say? Words coming up unbidden, words from a page we read together, *for by grace are ye saved,* and all that will come is this:

"We were friends, just friends." Words hanging in the air for them to do with what they please. You were just a dream I followed too far, the only proof I have that the last fifty years ever

happened

to her as if it really were an accident, telling the story again to this doctor leaning over her, staring at her eyes and nodding with an imperceptible slow twitch of his chin, the same way she told it to Tom and then the girls again in their turn, convincing herself a little more each time that the fragment of porcelain merely slipped and gouged her. With the television silenced, the girls have left the room again, in search of entertainment. Tom stands with his hands locked together over the crotch of his puffy khaki pants and observes the doctor in action, perhaps again out of purely technical curiosity, studying the methods of another type of professional. The key is to repeat the story exactly the same way each time, inserting a few details along the way to make it seem as realistic as possible without giving away the most important—and most subjective—detail: what went on in her head at the moment the "accident" happened. Who's to say but Holly what she was thinking, what swirling stream of thoughts was passing through her at that precise instant. Perhaps she did simply drop the jagged fragment or let it slip. The more she tells people this, the more convincing it seems.

"I'm going to shine this light in your eyes. It may be a little bright."

The doctor has the haggard look of someone who spends most of his life bathed in the fluorescent pallor of hospital rooms such as this. His hand comes close to Holly's face, flicking a beam of intense light into her eye.

"Try not to blink." He leans closer to her. She can see individual hairs tufting over the top of his earlobe, but otherwise she has been rendered blind by this light. She forces herself to obey his command, holding the eyelids open. His breath smells of garlic.

"Good." The light shifts to her right eye now, subjecting it to the same blinding brilliance. She cannot help but blink. But she resolves to keep the eyes open, and soon he retracts the light and tucks it away in the pocket of his corduroy pants. Beneath the veneer of his white lab jacket, the doctor is dressed more casually than Tom; beat up brown loafers, a golf shirt that has seen better days.

"Now," he says, standing up straight, "I want you to take your finger, your pointer finger, hold it out here like this, and touch it to the tip of your nose."

Holly sits up and feels her head swim. She holds her hand out in the distance like he showed her, and it seems very far away, an object disconnected from herself, almost beyond her control. She brings the hand back towards her face and to her great surprise finds that she misses the mark, touching just off to one side and grazing the wing of her nostril. In a way, this is funny. It reminds her of the time she was out with a guy named Ali about two years ago, maybe three, and they were coming back from some party near Eagle Crest Lake and the cops pulled him over and made him take a sobriety test. Sitting there with the blue and red lights of the cop car flaring against the dashboard, watching Ali stagger a few steps forward and then huff into the little tube they held up for him, she couldn't help but laugh at him. And now, here she is, failing a test of her own, one more in a long sequence of examinations she has not passed. She has never been good at complying with the requirements of life's institutions: school, church, marriage, things that require her to do things correctly. Things that require a certain amount of belief. Now the people in this hospital are checking to see what's wrong with her and are finding her deficient.

"Look straight ahead." The doctor moves his finger out to a place beyond her left ear. "Can you see this?"

"Yes."

"What about this?" The hand and finger have gone farther back, to a point where she thinks she can still see them, but maybe she is just imagining it.

"Yes. I think so."

"Good."

The nurse that came in before has returned, hovering at the end of the bed, waiting for the doctor to finish. Tom wants to say something, to exert his benevolent presence. "What are you finding, doc?"

The doctor ignores him. He takes Holly's hand firmly into his. "Now, I'm going to give your arm a little tug."

This seems strange—why would he do this? She holds her arm out directly in front of her, and he pulls on it. The arm feels loose and limp under his control, like a long damp towel being wrung out. She wants to pull her hand away from him, but he doesn't let go. Instead, he grabs her now by the elbow and tugs again. Her hand and wrist flop in response. More to the nurse than anyone else, he says, "We'll do a head CT. Maybe keep her overnight."

With this pronouncement, the doctor wheels about and hustles out of the room. Tom's question has remained unanswered. The nurse pokes the screen of a laptop computer several times with a plastic stylus, then trudges out as well, tugged along by the tidal weight of the doctor's last comment. Alone with Tom again, the translucent pain of Holly's headache shifts from one part of her skull to another, like one of those vivid jellyfish that bob and slither through the sea. She has been enveloped in the unfathomable workings of the hospital, in its mesh of strange people and procedures where time is beyond her control. The immediate future spreads out before her as a broad slippery mudflat, gray and wet, a place where minutes and hours blend together in a timeless mesh of faces floating above her, the faces of the doctor and Tom and the nurse interchangeable with others that have no features, dim ovals of blurred flesh. Oddly, Tom's voice seems to emerge from one of these blurred ovals.

"The doctor, before he came in here. He was asking me some questions."

There are always questions in a place like this. The object is always to try and pin people down, organize them into convenient sets of characteristics, points of data. "He thinks you may have a fractured skull." An image of the broken fragment of porcelain crowds into view, her own blood staining it. "He asked me what happened, whether it was an accident. As if I might have had something to do with it." There is a touch of indignance in this last phrase. "I said maybe it was from the fall, after you were cut. But I don't like making stories up."

He comes closer.

"Tell me what happened. Who was it? I'll slap a restraining order on him."

Holly can see now, in the dark crescent of space within the cuff of Tom's sleeve, a patch of black hairs that comes up and around the outside of his wrist. The hairs are coarse and dark, almost like pubic hairs, distinct from the pale down that covers the rest of his arm. Tom's upper lip juts out as he forms the words he is saying. "Did someone hurt you, or did you hurt yourself?" Then, as if there has been a skip in a phonograph record, another sentence comes out. "Listen Holly, I want to marry you." The sounds his mouth makes are separate from him, from his tongue and teeth and pink gums. The words hang there frozen between them, punctuated by the blip of the machine that tracks the involuntary squeezing of her heart. In a moment of clarity, Holly sees that this is one of Tom's tactics, a kind of negotiating ploy. He must do the same type of thing in his job. The statement is so absurd in this context that it cannot be taken seriously. And yet, it is out there. A position that has been staked out in the far distance, an objective he might some-day achieve.

Holly has a sudden vision of the series of meetings she and her former husband had to endure with the bland sorrowful minister who was going to marry them, in which he instructed them on the church's view of the mission they were about to undertake. She and Jake had been living together quite happily at the time, a fact that was known by the minister but never mentioned. These sessions were supposed to set up a frame-work of support and holy justification for the marriage, sancti-fying the bond that already existed between them.

"Tell him it's none of his business." She can only ignore what Tom said about marriage. She must push him away. Lying there in the bed, she feels tired and small. Her eyes want to close. "If he asks you again, tell him to go fuck himself."

Before Tom can respond to this, the nurse is back in the room once more, unannounced. Time in this place is carved into frail uneven segments drawn out by waiting. The nurse looks older now than when Holly first saw her. Her skin has the tough leathery gloss of a smoker. She sidles up to Holly and holds out a metal prong sheathed in plastic. "Open." The command is flat and direct, no explanation required. Holly has been given commands like this before. Opening her jaws this wide pulls the ache from the base of her head along the stretched muscles that run from her chin to the back of her skull. The nurse slides the prong in under her tongue, and Holly instinctively closes her lips on it, cold and hard. "Okay honey. Give me your arm."

Holly extends the arm that has been wounded, the one with the rusty bandage shielding her wrist. Gently, the nurse wraps Holly's biceps in a black plastic sheath, the velcro patches on either end catching and holding tight. The nurse steers a rolling tree of equipment with a digital readout connected to both the metal prong in Holly's mouth and the sheath on Holly's arm. She presses a button on the readout and the sheath springs to life, puffing up with air. Holly feels her arm locked in, compressed. The tips of her fingers tingle from lack of blood. Her mouth filled with the hard metal probe, her arm tethered to the box in the nurse's hands, she is fully under control. Tom's eyes are on her too, watching, waiting, narrowed and

clasping   her
hand, he leads her from the table to the ballroom floor, blending in with the others, together with the rest of them, flowing with the notes, the crisp notes of the horns threading their way among bare arms, drawing them onward, outward, apart and away, pulling together, pushing, twisting, unfurling apart again. The sinuous pitch of the clarinet sweeps up their spines, rotating slow, slow, grasping each other towards arching shoulders, backs supple and tense, but not really our music, this was left over from our parents and war days. Maybe they thought it would be more elegant, more in keeping with the final days of this place for tonight, but ours was new music never heard before, not this slow and subtle. Ours driven by loud drums and guitars, not this way of slowly building, quiet, hushed, then ris-

ing, lifting the couples paired one with another, each man with a
woman, each woman with a hand locked in hand approaching
cheek pressed to cheek. Hands on backs and shoulders, hands
held together wide and steering, pushing

together your things
and my things, his things and her things. She wants to show
him that all the erroneous, agglomerated stuff he has acquired
over the years can be easily carved up and divided, sold for cold
hard cash in an effort to make the impending move much eas-
ier. Her plan is to get rid of all the old possessions they have
accumulated and move back east with as little as possible.
Throw it all out. Declutter. The money they save on the move
will then be used to buy new things, new furniture and clothes
and housewares, once they settle in to the new house. New
glasses and plates and silverware. New bedspreads and sheets.
New everything, an experiment of hers, this new hard woman
who lives with him; she wants to show him that it all amounts
to nothing, all the detritus of the marriage that has built up over
the years.

But he loves these things he has worked so hard to buy. He
loves the king-sized bed she says is too cumbersome and heavy
to move. He loves his collection of old suit jackets and ties, the
clothes he wore to work each day, each tie gathering dust (for
no one wears ties any more) still connected to a set of workday
memories, places he went to, hotels and airports and three-
cocktail business dinners spanning decades by now. Some of
these ties go back to the Nixon administration. This gold one
with bold blue diagonal stripes is a perfect salesman's tie though

it has to be thirty years old if it's a day. He could wear this tie to next week's meetings and no one would blink an eye—though no one wears ties any more. That's what she said: "No one wears ties any more." So get rid of it. Throw it away. That is the assignment for the evening: Clear out his portion of the master bedroom closet. Sort through all the old clothes, the threadbare shirts and the dress shoes gathering dust, the athletic gear and the suitcases and the collection of photo albums stacked leaning against each other on the highest shelf. Go through all these things and decide what can be given away to the secondhand store or simply tossed in the trash to perish.

He cannot throw this tie away. He places it back on the rack and reaches for the portfolio where he keeps his work. Behind the network schematics for a food processing plant and the slick marketing brochures that tout the features of his company's products, the broad sheet of drawing paper has been waiting. He lays it on the lid of the plastic tub where the children's keepsakes are stored. There is not much light here: two fifty-watt bulbs, no windows, though the evening outside has faded into dusk and would not help much anyway.

The line he made is so faint, he has to squint to see it clearly. Though it does not reach the edges of the paper, it does divide the whiteness into two competing masses of empty space, the realm at the top of the page seeming to float on top of the smaller area below, the compressed field of blankness that already, with one stroke of his hand, seems to represent the earth. His hand grasps the pencil, touches it to the paper and draws it across, lightly, a thin scratching noise against the grain of the paper. A dim echo of the first line, an arc parallel to it and slightly above: the roofline of the building. Now another line, quickly, and another.

He stops for a moment and examines what he has drawn. He remembers now the unique and unnatural challenge of reducing a seen object to mere lines on a page. With a few strokes of the pencil, the image concealed within his head has materialized before him. When he entered the building, he would fly through the doors, those big glass doors, shoving them aside, and look for her, even as his pupils dilated to capture the hazy light of the lobby. Sometimes with Elmer, sometimes Louise. Sometimes all four of them together. Innocents. They were still innocents then. They had not yet made all of life's many mistakes.

From the doorway behind his head he feels a presence. Two eyes, boring into the back of his head, watching him work. In one deft movement, he lifts the lid of the rubber tub and slides the paper underneath it. Then he turns and sees Laura staring at him, her brown eyes blank, her mouth set in a disappointed slot.

"What are you doing?" She's holding the telephone away from her mouth, directing the words at him instead of the receiver. The implication of the question is that he is not doing what he should be, what she expected him to do. She tilts the phone half an inch higher and speaks into it. "Here he is . . . Do you want to talk to the bastard?"

Laura bends over and reaches the phone to him, her eyes screwed to the lid of the rubber tub and what lies beneath it. He sees in the glance she gives him everything that he hates about her: Her rigid focus on the list of tasks that is constantly circulating within her head, the relentless ticking of the clock inside her that urges her on, compelling her to nag him if a particular job she has decided he must do has not yet been completed; her unremitting concentration on the mundane details of daily life. Yet that had also been one of her chief attractions to him when they first met. He saw her as a challenge; he was always trying to show her how much he knew, impressing her with his knowledge and understanding of the world and its ways. She was so fixed on the brutal reality of each moment that he had to lift her above and away from it. He set out to prove to her that there was something more to life, entire oceans and continents far beyond her limited horizon, and in a few fleeting moments she did in fact acknowledge that there was something else out there.

"What's wrong with Mom?" The voice from the phone crackles and fades, the voice of his daughter.

"Your mother has decided that she doesn't like me very much." He tries to soften this, with Laura standing there directly above him. "She's all worked up about selling this house."

Laura's voice is raised, talking at the phone from a distance. "I don't appreciate your father's *insensitivity*." Trying to make herself heard from a few feet away, she's virtually shouting now. "I think he must be getting *senile*."

Did Abbey hear any of this, on the other end of the line? If she did, she gives no indication. "I wanted to see," she says, her voice clearer now as she has perhaps moved to a better spot for her cell phone's reception, "if you can come out to visit next

115

month. For Kelsey's birthday. Maybe the last time we have a big party for her. She'll be twelve, can you believe it?"

His granddaughter, turning twelve. He looks to see if Laura is still standing behind him, but she has gone, in search of another drawer to empty, another cabinet to clear. And this turns his mind back to the idea of leaving this house and all its memories behind, all the ghosts of their lives there together, all its cunning custom features they once found to be charming and useful but now merely bullet points on a listing sheet that might add up to a few more dollars on the asking price as calculated by the realtor. Why do they have to go? Why leave one place for another? Perhaps it is the idea of moving on to the next phase of his life that frightens him. Retirement, wide open, staring him in the face like a gaping starless sky. After that, only one final move, into a nursing home or directly into a plush wooden box.

To fight off these thoughts, he holds the phone to his face and speaks. "I don't know if we can make it. I've been on the road a lot, and your mother is having a real panic attack about selling this house. She's like a crazed animal about money right now."

"Why is she so upset?"

"She's afraid. She wants to get every last cent she can out of the house, and we found out today there are some problems, some things that might prevent us from putting it on the market. At least right away."

There is a pause on the line, a second of open air filled with the light crackle of the cell phone's intermittent reception. "What kind of problems?"

He doesn't want to go into the details. She doesn't need to be dragged into their problems. She has her own life to live, and they are her parents, the ones who are supposed to take care of her.

"Nothing that can't be fixed."

Then, in the gap his terse reply has left in its wake, he hears it, a sound beyond the muffled static of Abbey's bad connection: Another person's breath on the line. He can hear her, that shallow breath like the feeling of her eyes on his back, watching him draw, her presence over his shoulder has constantly defined him, the push of her wants and needs constricting him, dictating his actions. Her breath drawn in and released, saying nothing. Listening.

"Your father is getting senile," the other voice says, finally choosing to speak. "Your father, in his wisdom, decided to cancel the bug treatment for the house a few years ago, without telling me, and now the house is being *destroyed* by termites. Destroyed. And now, of course, when we need it, he can't put his hands on the homeowners insurance policy to see if we're covered." There is nothing he can say. She can go on like this for hours, ranting, this new liberated incarnation of Laura, telling him all the things he has done wrong in the past, all the things he has made her suffer through, all the things she is going to do to change it.

"I looked it up online, the damage these grotesque things can do. They can nest in the weight-bearing beams of a house and *devour* it. Thousands of dollars of damage. The house may be structurally unsound. This could literally eat up all the equity we have in the house. Our retirement money. We may not even be able to put it on the *market.*"

He envisions the termites eating into the wooden planks two stories below him that support his weight and the weight of the entire house. He sees them writhing in their hive, burrowing, as she put it, deeper into the grain of the wood. A slow process of rotting away. To him and to Laura, the termites forming their colony in the beams of their home is an act of unparalleled destruction. But he can see this, for a brief flashing moment, from the insects' point of view as well. Looked at from their perspective, these small disgusting beings building their hive are creating their own bit of order in the universe, fighting entropy in their own way. All life does that. He has to shake this perverse glimmer of logic from his head in order to speak.

"Laura, that's ridiculous. This house is worth five times as much as we paid for it. The market is so hot here, a few thousand to fix this won't hurt us. And it's probably covered by the insurance. We'll find out Monday when we call the title company."

"How do *you* know how much the house is worth? It could cost a hundred thousand dollars to repair it."

"Nonsense."

"You should have thought of that when you were saving a few bucks by canceling the exterminators."

There's that word she loves to use: Should. Always thinking about what must happen in order for her plans and her concept of the perfectly ordered world to take place. You should have done that. We should do this. You should get the oil changed in the car. You should clean out the gutters this weekend. You should really think about going to the doctor for that. You

should

have been here tonight with me again, one last time in this room, in this building where girls laughed, smoke gathered in the lobby, ringing out a sound from across the rooftops it came, the bells of St Monica's ringing out, the laughter raining down from the balconies. This life for you all dead and gone, but I kept you folded here inside me, I kept you locked within my heart, not really you but that one forgotten part of you is with me still, has been with me ever since, a fragment of us that never went away. He holds her adrift, floating, extending as far apart as they will ever be, for a shivering instant he holds her there locked together with his eyes. Why should I have kept myself sanctified for him? I might have had what they have, these two locking their eyes together. I might have had a separate life of my own, with children and grandchildren, and another who cares about me. But I chose to do this, enfolding myself together like a flower that closes against the cold.

But I did have something of a family too myself. He never knew it, but I did have Karl and Dennis those years when they lived with me, Karl so much older, nearly ten years older. His voice booming out across the heads in the pews, black backs of their heads riveted on the words he lashed out. *As for myself,*

119

brethren, when I came to you I did not come proclaiming to you the testimony and evidence or mystery or secret of God. His voice like a bass drum struck with a mallet, launching itself to the rafters, back from Philadelphia after Jessamine died to preach at St Monica's. I was there every Sunday for years, with the milky soft light through the stained-glass windows pouring down upon his face as the words hurried out like they were not his own, he was just a sounding board for giant strings that had been plucked. Still saying mass in Latin and living with me. Too old to be a brother, he seemed more like an uncle, but also what Tris never knew and I never told a soul, he was also like a husband and Dennis to me so much like a son. Dennis's head, his hair when I touched it, when I tucked the boy into bed; there is nothing so tenuous and innocent as the hair on the back of a young boy's head. I loved him like my own son, cut down without warning they said. His smile in the photograph I still have on the bureau in the back room, the room locked up. I never go there, filled with ghosts and mourning, locked up in the back of the house upstairs, that room where Karl slept each night in a single bed alone. Dennis's photograph, his smile, in his Army uniform.

We ate each meal as a family would, father, mother, and son together. And so, yes I did have a husband and a son, that has not been denied me in that sense. The Sunday after the message came, Karl still said mass, his voice resounding to the highest rafters. *Then He was praying in a certain place, and when He stopped, one of His disciples said to Him, Lord teach us to pray as John taught his disciples. And He said to them, when you pray say, Our Father who art in heaven, hallowed be Thy name. Thy kingdom come, Thy will be done.* He said it with a crack in his voice. *Thy will be done.* And the tears came to me and to others, to many others that day because they knew just as well that Dennis had been killed in the war, and the mourning was the end of us together. That booming voice of Karl's, those were the last words he ever preached. He said it that day, but that Sunday was the end of him and the end of us together. He loved his Dennis so much, and the Lord took him so young that Karl in his own way folded himself up in that bed in the back room. He went there and lay down and rarely left it in the months that came after. I fed him, brought him his food and drink, but it broke him, saying mass that day. He should have stepped aside, but he was a stubborn, deliberate man. He lay down in that bed in that room and never left, with Dennis smiling, staring at him. I grew to hate that room and closed it off, the door shut always against the ghost of him, always shut against that

bed she calls him to. How can she want to do this now, after all the acrimony between them? Her appetites have become like those of a man as the past few months have aged her, whittled her down to a hardness and ceaseless wanting. She calls him from the closet he has been cleaning, two piles of clothes heaped on the closet floor: one for the storage unit and one for the secondhand store. He knows the tenor of that voice, the way she called his name, lifting, with a question in it that quickly falls away. He sees her standing hunched over the bed naked, the flesh at the back of her thighs as slack as the blanket she lifts and lets fall again, slowly settling down upon a cushion of air between it and the tightly tucked sheets, her buttocks narrow as a boy's, the folds of loose skin where her belly used to protrude now hanging like a pouch as she stoops over and pulls the blanket taut at the head of the bed, pushing the blanket in between the box springs and the frame to make the bed the way she likes it, perfectly tight, everything sealed in.

Now she pulls the quilted comforter up to the headboard, her small breasts hanging limp as she smoothes out the wrinkles and props two pillows up, intent upon her work. Her nakedness is an indication of her mastery of him. Her focused disregard of his watching her a sign of his weakness. This is but another plan she is executing, an idea most likely conceived some time several days ago, while he was away on his trip, a task that took its place at the end of her long to-do list for this day. He could choose to ignore her, go downstairs and turn on the football game, open a beer. He was never properly fed this evening. A bowl of canned soup and a handful of pretzels have left him hungrier than ever. But this may be a chance to redeem himself, after everything that has happened with the house. He's surprised she would even consider it.

"Why are you making the bed?"

She doesn't look up. Walking to the dresser, she pulls open the drawer where the condoms are kept, confirming that he has guessed correctly. She takes one of the foil packets out of the box and leaves the drawer open, the big box of condoms crowded together with her silky underwear.

"I don't like to sleep on messy sheets, with the blankets all in a wad." Meaning he does. Implying that this is another failure of his. He can see her mind clicking like gears in a clock. This is another part of the plan, everything has been thought out: the closet will be cleaned, then we'll have sex, then I'll go to sleep. The sex is merely one step in the process. "It's been a while," she says—another accusation—marching up to him, naked, her breasts bare before him, so loose and limp that he has to avert his eyes and focus instead on the hand that has cupped itself firmly to the crotch of his jeans. Once she has decided to go through with something, she wants it to happen fast. At times he has to ask her to help him, paying extra attention with her hands or her mouth; he enters each encounter with her with no idea whether he will be up to the task. She pushes up on her toes in an effort to kiss him. Reluctantly, he lets her. She jabs her tongue between his teeth and the chalky taste of toothpaste presses against the remnants of the soup he ate.

Somewhere deep in his brain, a chemical mechanism is tripped: This woman, this hard little woman wants him. She fumbles with his fly and releases his mouth from the kiss. As she bends to her work, his mind lifts away from the presence of her and rises to a place somewhere near the spackled rafters in the ceiling, away from her and outside himself, a place where he has been reduced to pure sensation, a tiny rip in the fabric of time; an opening for everything that ever was him to drain out of. For a long moment he floats there, apart from himself, forever beyond the distant antipathies obtaining a scaffold for his soul. The room is gone and the ceiling, all gone for a moment, then—she is back and he is. She is Laura and he is everything he has ever been once again, tucked inside himself once more and here, in this room they will soon be abandoning.

She tugs on his arm, indicating it is time to join her in bed. He knows what to do now—their routine in these matters has been choreographed quite precisely over the years. As she turns down the sheets of the bed she has just made he must quickly, quickly take off his clothes. In bed now, they assume the accustomed positions, on their sides, her head over his, her mouth searching. "Mmm . . . " she says. "This is good."

No, don't talk, he thinks. Talking brings him back to her. He feels himself start to fade, and decides to shift positions. It's now or never. He lets go of her and starts to climb on top.

"Not so fast." She knows exactly what her next move will be, and so does he. She tears and uncrinkles the silver foil wrapper of the condom and subjects him to the indignity of rolling it on, her hands tugging expertly at the rolled rubber end. This is another one of her new proclamations, the condom, after years of lovely unrestricted sex courtesy of the pill, she has declared that she will no longer soak her body in unhealthy, unnatural chemicals for him—she claims that she very well may have given herself some kind of cancer, just so he can have an extra measure of feeling. So, despite her dwindling post-menopausal body, she has insisted that he use "protection." Protection from what? He couldn't get her pregnant if he tried. Maybe she suspects him of being unfaithful, all those long lonely nights on the road. It's a valid concern. But he has come to believe that it is more a matter of her staking a claim to her body, delineating a territory that he no longer owns. This is mine once again—once and for all. You can visit me here, but only on my terms.

He can hardly blame her for this. He has scorned her for considering this act to be merely one more chore on her list, but it is, indeed, work. When she first surprised him by bringing home the big box of condoms with the shadowy forms of two lovers silhouetted on the flat golden lid, he marveled that she had the guts to even carry such a thing to the checkout lane of the drugstore, and he noted that this particular brand advertised in large clinical lettering that the condoms are RIBBED, FOR HER PLEASURE. As she tugs the rubber tight, he can discern the tiny notched bumps that constitute the "ribs," and he doubts they give her any pleasure at all. Finishing, her eyes momentarily flash up at him. For an instant, he sees her there, a person inside those two dark holes; a person who must eat and sleep and dream each day just as he does, the person who all those many years ago cast her lot with him and has had to endure his many faults and shortcomings. For a moment, he sees the person there, behind those tawny eyes, who clings to hopes and cringes in fear of imagined catastrophes, who goes about each day with her own familiar will to live and carry on, and he cannot help but love her, as he always has, for being the one whom he somehow convinced to join him and never leave his

side of the room is nearly empty, a lot of the people over towards the bar now that the band has been playing a while, only the die-hard dancers still out there, the rest of them standing in twos and threes with drinks in their hands, talking, waving tumblers of whisky or gin or rum in the air. Tris would be taller than most, his head towering over the others, easy to spot. His high forehead, cropped dark hair. I think of him as he was and not as he might be or must be now. I think of him as that young boy really in the hammock with me, or the one who dashed across the lobby, eyes lit up with laughter, always laughing about some joke he just heard, always making up something to smile about. But maybe there wouldn't even be any hair any more, maybe glasses or some other change I wouldn't even recognize, somebody altogether new. An arm, a hand brushes against my sleeve. Is it him? Turning, expecting to see him there, his dark hair and eyes like gimlet shimmers of blue. He must be, but no, this is someone I never have met before, touching my sleeve.

"Would you care to dance?" The voice dry and cracking, breaking away at the soft last sound of the word, but the hand stays there still, fingertips pressed through the fabric, pressing against my skin. How long has it been since any man touched me? There is no answer, no sound I can make. Now his hand takes my hand and holds it, leading me to the center of the floor like Elmer leading me across the street against the danger of traffic, or me leading that girl, and now his arms, his arms around me, his hand touching, testing the small of my back, guiding me. The people, their faces hanging suspended, floating this way and that, turning aside and swishing.

"I bet you don't remember me." Sound of the trumpets flaring against the cry of the hollow clarinets.

"No, I must say I'm sorry, I don't."

He smiles and the cheeks tipped with red rise up.

"I knew you wouldn't. We hardly knew each other then, but here we are fifty years on. Jimmy Boyle," he says, letting me drift farther apart, releasing me, maybe to get a better look. "I used to do the paper route on Dearborn Street, all around St Monica's." And his face transposes into another, into a boy with a short-billed cap sprinting across the two-tiered stubby lawns of the street, flipping the rolled-up paper onto the porch with a slap. Sometimes Father would curse him for hitting the milk box or missing the porch entirely.

"I do remember you. You used to be so shy with your black leather collection book, especially when Louise came to the door. I remember once you tripped on the milkbox and nearly broke your neck down those stairs, backing away and staring at her." Should I tell him I still live in the very same place? Probably the only one in this building who still lives in the house they grew up in.

"We all stared at her. My God, she was a knockout."

"Yes, she was, wasn't she?" And she knew it, and made sure everyone else did too. He lets me drift a bit farther away, as if to get a better look at me, appraising. No one has looked at me like this in forty years.

"Well, none of us are knockouts any more." He draws me in closer, pressing his beery breath against my cheek. "Even Louise must be old and gray I imagine."

Yes, I want to say. Yes, she is. She lives in an old farmhouse, dingy and dark and just as alone as I am. I may have had a lonely life, but mine was never as sad and tangled up in tears as hers. All of her husbands and children, what a mess she made of it. Her good looks nothing more than a beacon calling shipwrecks towards her.

127

"She's doing very well, a writer living near Bremerton. A lovely little place she has out in the woods near the state park." He brings me closer, still pressing the hard starched collar of his shirt against my chin. His mouth, his lips are close, close, maybe he thinks I'm her. Or maybe just pressing himself against a relation of hers is enough for him, his

arms clasping him to her, he feels himself open up into pure sensation again, his self falling away, floating upwards into nothingness, a big open hole ripped from the fabric of the sky, her arms pulling him down into a pit that never ends, a space as loamy and wide as the earth itself, smooth and distended, plunging to the horizon and beyond. But she has shielded herself from touching him, he can feel himself in her but cannot feel her, it is the same as having her watch him draw, she will not let him

feel his hands but not just his hands, his fingertips touching me, and not just touching me, caressing me, exploring my back. I shrink down, I close myself. When Louise told Father that we were to meet under the clock that day, when she told him that we were together in that way, she ripped you apart from me forever, she did the cruelest thing a person ever could. Her jealousy of me and of you came full circle after years of hating us and what we had together. She could have had anyone she wanted, yet she could not stand the thought of us together. When she told him that we were together so young, too young, she ripped you apart from me forever. But we were not really, that's what I told Father that evening when I arrived home after you didn't show, and Father screamed, my God, he never raised his voice to us but that night he screamed and scared Mother so she drove him from the house. And then he used that word, he said it to Mother when it never really was that. We never did that together, but he said it, screamed it for all the house to hear, and from that moment on I folded into myself, I renounced you and any other, folded into myself to keep it from ever happening. When he screamed that word and Mother shoved him out the back door screaming, I said to myself at that moment never, never again will I let someone

touch him there, she does this sometimes to tweak him, to get an extra rise out of him, one of her tricks, but the thought has entered his head that she will not let him feel and thinking this thought or any thought for that matter other than pure loose and otherworldly feeling has sent him back into his head, his self and her self, separate and apart and vexed by the acrimony of earlier this evening so he must think of another woman; he can feel himself failing. The woman from the television news darts into his head, her lips moving slowly, mechanically, pronouncing her words of doom. She is perfect, too perfect, her face and hair an abstraction, she talks, and the crazy nonsense letters scroll across the screen beneath her, and the child trapped pinned beneath the rubble, she is too perfect, she is death. He keeps going but has to shift positions, move his arm a bit to get the blood moving; it was starting to tingle. He twists his head across her shoulder beneath him and opens his eyes again and sees the yellow wall gleaming beyond the edge of the bed, the yellow wall that she once painted of the house they will be leaving soon.

There, grasping for his attention, is a scuff mark on the wall, a smeared green streak that he never thinks of but knows quite well; he has seen it a thousand times through the course of his daily existence here, a mark left by a ball the children must have been throwing when they used to jump on the bed, a scuff mark from one of his racquetballs the kids used to steal and heedlessly carom around the house. He feels himself dwindling, the barrier between himself and her is as much of a distraction as this green mark. He must keep going, he must think of someone else. He envisions the woman in the hotel elevator who offered herself to him, who made that remark—what was it, what did she say?—he cannot remember now, something about being trapped in the elevator with him, and this is also no good, a vision of the two of them on the dirty hard floor of the elevator, so he goes back to her, to that impalpable remnant of earliest and purest experience, her warm presence next to him under the blankets, her breath upon his ear exciting him, the presence of a girl in the bed with him enough to make him

hard to tell where his hand ends, where it stops it blends into my back, into me, and that is why I fold myself up. His hand pressing firm against the small of my back is too low, pressing me, leading me this way and that. Never again, I said, never again will I let someone touch me, entwine their life into mine. I have made myself inviolate and pure, so now this man must not, must never do what you must have wanted to do, though Father never believed me. He did know that you must have wanted to and I must have wanted to, so I closed myself off forever so he would know that what he thought about me was not true. I have folded myself up forever, and though his hand is cool and easy to let go, I have closed myself off waiting for you. I have done this thing that is no thing for years upon years, have denied and maintained and kept a completeness whole without any other unto myself, so not even you or any other will defile me, not even you nor any

other, that was the thing, he has latched onto it now, having a separate other person next to him who was of the other sex or not so much sex but just different really. He didn't even know what sex was at that age but just different, a girl in the bed with him bouncing around. They were supposed to be taking a nap so the neighbor woman who was watching them along with Elmer and Louise, the whole wrecking crew, as the parents used to call them, over at Irene's for the afternoon, and after she had had enough of their running around and screaming, tearing through the house, she simply sent them all upstairs to take a nap, though they must have been at least seven or eight years old, with no direction as to which rooms or beds they were to sleep in, just a weary solemn command to go upstairs, the lot of you, and settle down and take a nap. And Elmer tried to first organize them into some game, hide and seek or Indians, but Louise, haughty Louise, who loved to torment him by sabotaging his plans, refused to go along.

Louise retreated to the mysterious room in the back of the house where a single narrow bed was kept but no one ever

slept, and Elmer in the middle room where the sewing machine
and all of Irene's colorful ranks of bobbins whirred, and that
left him with her at first just bouncing and jumping on the big
queen bed; but then, both of them under the covers, telling stories, talking about who knows what. Laughing—always laughing. And then a hand maybe her hand first, touching. That was
it, just a touch, but enough to send him now forward into fullness driving into her swept along by crystal pure revelation of
another—any other—and the other in the bed beneath him
whom he is touching has become not just anyone but has become

me, that is all I have left, only me, because he will not
come now, he will never touch me again, and perhaps he never
did love me. This beery old man with his hand on my back is
not him, and he never will be. There is only one thing to wait
for now that you have not come. I pull my head away from his
hard crisp collar, from the warm torrent of his breath in my ear.
He will never touch me any more than this, and not even Tris
will touch me, only one more thing to wait

for this one thought
has opened him up and engulfed him enough that there is no
more thought remaining, only a parallel track of sensation
spreading wide beneath him dredged up from the depths of a
bed, a hammock, a tumble on the ground, and her bending over
to pick something up off the gritty summer sidewalk of the
plaza outside the theater.

She bent over and he saw for a quick tender moment the
dark gap of blackness between her breasts, the lowcut summer

dress revealing a furrow that brings him into the pull of great nothing spread wide beneath him, ever wider the opening goes, in the hammock curled against him her warm summer form of a girl, knees knocking together as they swung, a hand just resting there in the space between the

darkness coming, only the full ripe darkness coming to meet me now, not you nor anyone else, not even the gentle slue of the hammock in summer, the giant branches of the pinoak and the moon swinging high against the dusk, not even that can stop the darkness, though in darkness and in light I am even yet

becoming more and more a blankness and always finally letting

go and finding there is everything and nothing

more to do than let these big husky men in their pale blue surgical scrubs wheel her down the waxed corridors of the hospital towards exactly what she does not know. As the lights sail by above her in a kind of rhythm, Holly imagines a melody the glaring fluorescent tubes could produce, a steady procession of tones so monotonous only a machine could generate it; when she hums it in her head, there's not enough variation for the tones to have been struck by a human hand. They carefully edge around a corner, then two bumps as the wheels trundle over a threshold and into a quieter ward than before. Fewer people walking here, it feels as if she has truly entered the depths of the building, the place where the serious work of the hospital is accomplished. One of the orderlies stares at her breasts through the flimsy hospital johnnie. He can probably see the shadowy outlines of her nipples protruding. Go ahead and get a good look. Won't be the first, won't be the last.

An angled hallway leads off to one side. They slow for a moment, then bump open a door. Each room in the hospital seems to have its own inhabitants, who comfortably occupy their niche within the larger environment. This place echoes with the cool, antiseptic flavor of a large tiled bathroom, clean and cheerful, with a staff of technicians apparently awaiting her arrival. Their task completed, the lead orderly, the one she thinks of as her driver, scribbles a note on a clipboard and leaves her in the hands of her next set of caretakers. She hasn't had this much attention lavished on her since the days of her pending graduation from high school, when the family feared she would not graduate, would do instead something drastic like drop out and run away from home with her boyfriend or get arrested for smoking dope on the school grounds. Now a trim woman in yellow scrubs smiles at Holly and tells her they are going to perform what she calls a short "procedure."

"All you have to do is lay on your back and remain perfectly still." She says this in a way that makes it sound as if it will be harder to accomplish than it should. And then Holly sees why. After tugging the IV needle out of her arm and patching the hole with a gauze bandage, the technician helps Holly sidle onto a plastic ledge covered with a band of paper. This ledge juts out from the circular opening of an imposing machine that looks like an oversized dryer in a laundromat with glowing blue lights inside it.

"Lie back and get comfortable. We're going to take a look and see what's going on." Holly allows her head to sink into an overstuffed pillow while the technician pulls a thin sheet over her waist. Then the technician puts her hands on either side of Holly's head and maneuvers it the way Holly would tilt the head of one of her own customers during a cut. "We need you to look straight up and hold perfectly still for just a minute or two while the scan takes place. It may seem like a long time, but it's really only a few seconds. The bed will move you into the device automatically, and the X-ray sensors will move across your head, taking thin cross-section pictures." She places a kind of collar over Holly's neck; the collar tips Holly's chin up and holds it in place. "Then the computer will put these slices together to give us a very detailed picture of the whole."

Holly imagines the computer arranging delicate slices of her brain, its structures and synapses marred by her many indiscretions over the years. In her drug-induced bewilderment, she wonders whether they can make a mistake, putting the slices together in the wrong order somehow, converting her into a completely different person. Of course they can. Hospitals, or rather the people who work in them, make mistakes all the time, administering the wrong medications, switching the wristbands on newborn infants, sending them home to the wrong parents and wildly disparate future lives. This idea takes hold and evolves into a wish for something very much like this to happen; a mistake that would wipe all the mistakes of the past away.

135

"Now hold still. Take a deep breath and relax." The technician adjusts the position of her head one last time, fluffing the pillow up around her. "Just re-*lax*."

The hard platform her body rests on begins moving, slowly, almost imperceptibly slow. "Most people like to close their eyes during the procedure. A lot of people doze off and take a short nap." Holly finds this suggestion incredible. This rigid pallet she is lying on is more uncomfortable than the floor. She can feel the individual bumps of her spine pressing against it, like knobs on the trunk of a tree. And now that it is time to hold still, she is overwhelmed by an urge to twist her head to one side, rebelling against the impervious grasp of the collar tucked under her chin. It has always been this way—whenever someone tells her to do something, she has a powerful impulse to disobey and do the exact opposite.

But she keeps her head still, heeding the words of the technician if only to avoid what she guesses must be the result of any movement: an image of her brain that is scrambled or distorted in some manner. A few inches above her head, the lip of the circular opening to the machine approaches and passes slowly by, absorbing her into it, accompanied by a deep, nearly inaudible humming. Slowly, ever more slowly, her entire head and neck are consumed by the machine. Though her legs and torso extend freely into the open air of the examination room, as her shoulders approach the opening of the machine, the ledge shudders and she has the sensation of being entirely swallowed up by this humming metal box. Now a circular band within the tube begins to spin at an incredible speed, causing the hum that surrounds her to go up in pitch as it carves out a tiny cross section, a picture more finespun and meticulous than any ever taken of her. She closes her eyes to block this image and a vision of Tom sweeps over her, Tom hovering by the hospital bed, his round face etched with a look of concern; Tom holding the door for her on a date, bringing her elaborate gifts she can never live up to, enclosing her within his suffocating attentions, incorporating her into his pleasant but conventional life. Marriage to Tom would be like this, like sealing herself in a box.

For a few moments she allows her eyes to remain closed. Perhaps she does indeed sleep, as the technician recommended. How much time has passed? Two minutes, ten? She does not know. Without a known impulse from her, her eyes are open again, confronted by the harsh white roof of the cylinder, a few inches from her face. A thought comes to mind, prickling between her ears as if it has been transmitted by the high-pitched buzzing of the machine: *They will never be satisfied.*

The words linger, twisting around on themselves, coiling into a ball. She wonders whether the machine can register any of her thoughts; at the moment she is thinking this, the machine is taking another slice of her head, transcribing the exact structure and contents of the brain. She has convinced herself there is a great deal of truth to this statement: They will never be satisfied, the lawyers like Tom, the doctors and nurses. Her mother. The ones who are always probing and measuring her. The old woman who watched the girls last night and gave her that momentary look of disdain. They see everything; they know.

CR

I LAY MYSELF down in the garden, the garden will keep me whole. I lay myself down in the garden, the garden will keep me sanctified and whole. And Enrique, God bless him if he ever thought to wake up on a Sunday morning and roust his family to church, might look out from the back kitchen window and see me lying here in this mouldering damp plot of earth and wonder what the crazy old gringo lady has gone and done now. But he never does get them up and out to church, though the bells of St Monica's are loud enough when they call the early mass to make the sashes rattle. He sleeps right through it, up past midnight, up when I got home last night with his three fat children watching television too loud, and even the bells of the second mass only wake him up and get him to the porch in his t-shirt and baggy sweatpants reading the paper with his hair standing on end. So Enrique will not see me, nor anyone else even if they happen to look out from the second-story windows of the houses on either side. They will see now that I have crouched down bearing my weight on the butt of my hands in the dirt and lain myself, my heavy decrepit body, down in the dirt, still damp, wet with dew.

There is no one left to see me, for I am covered up now in the flowers of my garden, in the tender tall fronds of the snap-dragons and cone flowers, tall stalks of their stems lifting all around me, a forest from the red dusk globes of the cone flowers draping over me, a canopy of loose amethyst umbrellas. The snaps on their gabbling stalks, luminous, lavender and bronze, they cover me up, they genuflect and shield me, tired and still empty where I was ever hollow from lack, like a seed, like a grain of wheat falling into the damp earth, fallow, slow. Slow in the weight of me, all encompassed now in this great ungainly husk, still sanctified and whole, the entirety of my burden still sanctified and whole.

Was there ever one moment when I could have let go of my penitence, my impudent idea of showing, always showing him that—no—that is not what I was, that is not what I did. I am instead this: An emblem of forsaken need. When he said to me, *well, if you're not going to get a man, you have to get a job,* dry and hollow I became out of spite of him, of them, of you, Tris, yes you. I said, no, I will show you I never was what you thought of me. I never did that, and sure enough here I am with no one left to witness it but the canopy of leaves dumbly filtering the light, only this, Elmer's garden now mine as well and the great pinoak still here, still observant now as it once was of the girl I was before, when I was still light enough and free and not defined by a lack, by the weight of a lack drawn upon me. And blanketing like a hollow in my chest, I went about my business, my job, my chores, my meals, my life sideslipping the hollow every day and night, circumscribing the lack. Yet I did have things, I had many things in life to reprise me, to satisfy and drag through justifying days. They never left me, this great husk the body is a plenitude of pleasure, so who's to say that one is more preferred above another? Whole afternoons I ate and ate, I soaked in television, and these things are probably superior because they are pleasures of one's own, they are only unto me contained within that hollow, and did he not say that any one who loves his life will lose it, and anyone who hates his life in this world will keep it to life eternal?

I had no regard for my life here on earth. He said it and yes, Karl would agree. He who hates his life in this world preserves his life forever and ever. I only did what ever it was that proved convenient. I circumscribed my self, my daily coming and going, ever smaller, folding in upon my self. Karl would agree, he would see it now as sanctified and whole. When he came here from Philadelphia with Dennis, he pried my life open gently, like petals of snaps, and let me have companionship, in his authority it was not wrong.

Those years with him and with Dennis were enough to let me know that even a lack is something too, even this hollow is enough to keep my self vigilant to sacrifice, to maltreat, to proficiently maintain the lack and hollow is enough to pinion a semblance of living, to promise myself what he promised me too, which is another chance at longing, another evidence of his love, his beauty, his sin. In the cast of pewter light filtering through the August sky cloudspun and dulled, Elmer, your garden is still lovely. You would be happy to know it. Even the colors filtered through the Sunday pewter morning light. He was praying in a certain place. He said to them, when you pray his last sermon, and the light filtered through St Monica's windows, lavender and bronze, his last sermon and mine here.

Will they call her about the hair? They should. I have not left much, and neither have I asked for much. They should call her, and she should do it, in case. It is one last vanity, but it is not much. They should do it in case you Tris—in case one last time. But the porcelain vase is broken, the beautiful vase I threw, it flew, I did it myself against the wall, and shattered. It flew into a bright star of fragments, the fundament, the firmament, the first and the last and the moment is broken, never one whole together again. Ever here and ever smaller, folding myself in the wainscoting a crack and the fragments scattered in porcelain dust on the floor. Darkness and shadow creep from the leaves, interweaving the pewter Sunday sky.

All is alike, all is invisible, invincible, it creeps among me, a joy secure or neverlasting, on through the world the brilliant bright gong of the second mass bells sounding, sounding, they will ever let them weep. By God's decree, by the firmament, the fundament, the fragments of light and space filtered through lavender and bronze. He let go of me, he let go of us all, he let us fall until he was praying in a certain place, he said to them lavender and bronze, sanctified and

whole segments of time have been compressed into moments such as this, moments in which the hastening procession of evenings and mornings and afternoons one beyond another and the events they contain have been distilled into a finely grained, telescopic awareness of truth: This is the way things always have been and ever must be. He turns away from his work beneath the sink and glances over his shoulder at Laura in her terrycloth robe as she sets his plate of eggs on the table next to the paper and juice. From his position crouching on all fours, Laura with her back to him and towering above is captured in an essential pose of wifely endeavor, placing the meal she has just cooked for him on the table. The slight curve of her less than ample backside exaggerated by leaning over tugs at him with a distant resonance of the night before. He carefully returns his head to the crowded cavern of space beneath the sink where the line to the faucet has been leaking. Raw chemical smell of various liquid soaps and cleansers undercoats the sour tang from a can of rancid cooking grease she saves here. At the joint where the line attaches to the faucet hardware, a reflective sheen of liquid emerges and gathers into a solemn tear-shaped drop that eventually generates enough mass to detach itself and land with a light and merry plink in the metal mixing bowl he has placed on the floor of the cabinet to catch it. The entire process takes about seven seconds. Not a great deal of water, but enough to do damage over time.

With the loose precision of a practiced hand, Tris slots the head of the Stillson wrench over the joint, prodding the oily thumbscrew to clamp the jaws against the fixture. If they weren't about to sell this house, he would replace the warped and waterstained wood at the bottom of the cabinet. As it is, he has decided to wait until the inspection. If they note it and ask for it, he can repair it then. No sense spending time or money on something that may not matter; it can merely be lumped into the odds and ends they will cover by tossing an extra thousand or fifteen hundred dollars to the buyers at closing. Dollars on paper they never really had and never will see. But this can be repaired, this leak. This can be easily repaired and so can the damage the termites have done, whatever it may be. Rotting boards, corroding pipes, water seeping through broken ceramic tiles high above his head; mildew blanching the carpet by the door to the garage: These are of no concern. They can all be replaced and repaired—every last nail of the house can be. He keeps trying to tell her: There is a buyer out there waiting for this house to come on the market, and the buyer is not buying boards and beams, plumbing and wiring. They are buying their own preconceived idea of this place—the sun that bears down on the swimming pool in the waning afternoon, the view across the valley towards the dusky smog-blurred mountains. The Spanish mission feel of the houses stacked like dominoes against the side of the hill. When the buyer walks through the sliding glass doors to the patio and hears the quiet slosh of water spilling into the pool from the hot tub with the high clear light of the garden gleaning in the arbor, then, only then, will the house be sold. And none of the rest will matter.

"Everything can be fixed," he says, calling out to her from the recessed echoing space under the sink. "Even the termites."

Her reply comes back at him like a shot.

"You wouldn't know the truth if it hit you in the face."

The woman is dense, bitter and dumb. She carries her practical negative thinking around with her and waves it like a banner to proclaim how much more sane she is than anyone else around her. She likes to prove her point and always, always must have the last word. These things he has known for years coalesce into a vision that finally clouds and obscures the idealized remains of his earliest attraction to her. Surely that idea of her he created when they first met must have been based in some reality—an elegant, attractive woman imbued with the easy grace of an upper middle-class childhood—but over the years it has been corroded by exposure to words such as the ones just now, choked by a slow process of oxidation, building up layer upon layer. That old Laura is gone, replaced by this indignant, severe, worrying person. She is gone now.

He clenches his fist around the handle of the wrench and pushes it away from him, locking the seal of the joint tight. It closes shut with a creaking groan of metal upon metal. The final drop of water forms at the lip of the seal, its source shut off once and for all. He watches the water shimmer there, a layer of liquid pulled downward into an elongating sphere, a tiny mountain growing down from the sky. A piece of him is dying. A piece of him

falls broken into darkness blown upon me, rushing into an empty night, suffocating and vacant. The clear cold nothing ever growing, rushing millions down around a doorway, until there is no anywhere or anymore. This is the death of the body.

I am swimming rigid, rolling in ink, amidst the weary crushing rocks which shimmer down upon me, pressing all my adoration out. Clocks unravel the sea of cherished space, flat upon the vast and looming fundament, beyond what never was or claimed to be, gone to cold and deep and empty rendering. My very same releasing globe of Spirit grows as vast as every spreading galaxy beneath the spiral night askew. Passing noiseless ocean floor, floating in the gems of sinking waves of sun, askant and bloodless beams, never splendid, never silent. Swirling wisps of smoke surround me as I fall through this frightful dark and suffocating place, vacant and abstaining.

A hand, formless and opaque, cold and clutching at the top of my head and pulling me out into spinning majesty, pulling me out of the lifeless veil. The hand that grasps and bodily pulls away my form and essence, beyond a great and desolate wind and leaving behind the jaw-muscles, the clenched and shivered form in numb pneumonia. The hand keeps pulling, clutching me cold through the top of my head, stretching beyond a ceaseless ringing as of church bells, pealing noise profound. The crucial last beginning and no end, the spinning of all colors. Climactic peals of dirges, arpeggios of meaning, an idle chorus wild beyond all keening.

And so the names of all the angels sing. Asrael and Jezrael and Uriel and Jesus, all spinning tight into one sound, unspeakable and all consuming, stretching me out beyond the lifeless veil. Not touching yet not leaving, part of me still pegged in time, in one place and another, the hand that stretches me spreading wide a cord, a shimmering diastema, clear and smooth. This taffy cord of shivering light releases and snaps, returning part of me to my body, to my skin and hair and veins, part falling loose to nothing.

This glossy night unraveling is the death of the body. A cunning dimmed evasive hand pulled back and parted glossy night, oppressing the hollow stamp of my fear. Arpeggios are broken chords: Release the polished pearls, dissolving sound. I draw near to birds ensnared within a wall of galleries that rise like towers upon towers, traversing stars and suns and moons. My hands fall apart, they flutter like wings and flail apart, unbound from prayer, unbound from full and fleshly feeling.

The world has fallen away and with it every fearful stunning net and snare. The bells celestial rip the lap, the arm, the lip. Forlorn and spiral dwelling, cast about and throw the pieces round the vaulted stars so cold and dim and few.

This wretched scourge of wind now carries me onward to another place. This unyielding wind that whistles along, snapping, flapping, undulating wires, the wind rips loose the bonds, the lacquered surfaces, the inlaid neon tubing tied and tortioned into knots arrayed along a grid. This is the death of the body, ripped asunder now by wretched scourge of wind. I disappear on swift dark motions, tired and shaking through the doubtless reckoning of night.

A piece of me, those several million pieces fall apart and glide beneath a dim horizon never seen by light-winged smoke or thought or word. A broken shell of porcelain time betrayed, each second split apart, each second drenched and sucked into the sea of nothing ever seems as bad after he leaves the house for a while and escapes the confining rigor of her frustration. Each time, after a bit of unguided reflection, he comes to understand that it is merely her frustration with him simply being the way he is that leads to her bitter outbursts. After he has driven around the neighborhood or to the auto parts store or the coffee shop and had time to make this realization once again, he is then able to decide calmly and without remorse that he cannot change, that these outbursts and her grievance towards him will continue as long as they remain together. She would be frustrated with anyone. This is the conclusion he reached at some point early in their marriage. Anyone who wasn't her, who didn't do things exactly as she would have them done, who didn't share her viewpoints or accede to them would sooner or later infuriate her. Early on, in the days of their first studio apartment back east, he made an attempt to fold his clothes the certain way she recommended, to care as much about the tidiness of the place, to let her win every disagreement. But it didn't last. It couldn't. At some point, he simply had to be who he was or get out. And she has been struggling against this with him ever since.

"I must do what I must do."

Tris says this to no one in particular; he startles himself when he realizes he has spoken the words aloud and sees a woman across the aisle fingering the chain of a lighting fixture look up at him and stare. The woman startles him even more by being exceedingly attractive, peering over her shoulder at him from her position squatting down to examine what looks to be a dining room lamp relegated to a lower shelf of the massive hardware store—or, home improvement center. They don't call them hardware stores anymore. By squatting down on her haunches and bending forward to get a closer look at the lamp, the waist of the woman's tight-fitting blue jeans has buckled out to reveal the frilled elastic band of her underwear as well as a sizable swath of the creamy smooth skin of her lower back. This, combined with the perfect double roundness of her bottom and the flashing of her eyes, provokes him to return her stare for a moment longer than his embarrassment would have otherwise allowed. That skin . . . soft and pliable. Perfectly pale. The moment stretches, edging to the verge of discomfort. Finally, he turns away, repelled by her continuing closeness.

At the end of the aisle is a display selling children's books. It used to be that he could come to a hardware store and be consoled by the rough oily smells of sawdust and paint, soldering irons and forty pound bags of true-green fertilizer. Now every thing is everywhere. He once came to this mega-store when Laura was out of town with her friends and cobbled together dinner for himself from the two aisles of packaged processed foods near the checkout. Beautiful women such as the one he just passed have invaded this place, goaded into becoming erstwhile carpenters and plumbers by cable television shows that glorify and simplify the burdensome chores of remodeling and maintaining a home. Whole networks are now devoted to what were once dreaded mundane tasks. Yet there are still sections of the store where women rarely venture. He knows of an aisle— and this is one of the advantages of the modern big box retailer—that contains nothing but plumbing valves. Valves for pipes; a huge aisle with stacks and stacks of them, all makes and models.

He passes by an area with a selection of monstrously large gas grills. One Jen-Air model employs a 68,000 BTU burner. The cardboard sign propped on the open grilltop boasts of a 946 SQUARE INCH COOKING SURFACE. You could roast a whole pig on it. Beyond this, a snack bar with a cordon of vending machines beckons. He didn't eat the breakfast she set before him. But he avoids the candy bars and sodas and heads directly to the aisle he wants. AISLE 18 – PUMPS VALVES PIPES.

Tris has been fascinated by the dynamics of fluids since he was in college, the way things flow from one place to another, the swirling patterns of clouds on satellite pictures of weather, color infrared photos of the flow of water in rivers with their evasive, recursive coils and bends. He picks up a Threaded End 1 ¼" Industrial Ball Valve and hefts it in his hand. The metal is slippery, cold. In a way, he thinks, human beings are like valves for deflecting energy. Like the jet engine on the plane he contemplated yesterday, itself a giant valve, we suck in food, water, oxygen, and convert them into motion.

From the hip pocket of his jeans, a poignant jumble of classical notes emanates, muffled by fabric. He hopes it isn't Laura, though apologizing this soon would be unlike her. He flips the phone open and sees it is Hal Pope, his disgruntled customer in New Jersey, and decides to answer. What the hell . . . may as well take his medicine now. There is no weekend in this business any more.

"Tris Holloway." He answers the phone as if he doesn't already know who's calling, as if it is a Monday morning, not Sunday. A decade or two ago, most God-fearing Americans would have been expected to be in church right about now.

"Yeah Tris, hey. Hal Pope here."

"Hal. Good to hear from you. How's it going out there?"

Tris mentally cringes, expecting the worst. An image flashes through his head of a warehouse full of thawing food that his server should have been monitoring, releasing its foul odor of decay.

"Fantastic. I just wanted to let you know, you bailed my ass out the other day. Your guy, Teddy. He got the sonofabitch running again in less than ten minutes. You know, I have to say we don't usually get someone busting their balls for us like you guys. And when we do . . . well, I just wanted to thank you."

For now, Tris thinks. For the moment. Just wait; there is a time element to everything, an expiration date. The system is working now, but it will falter again at some point. We see the other three dimensions clearly, height and width and length. We see the color and texture of things; we feel and hear and smell them. But we don't see time. Well, we do see it, when we allow ourselves to see change. Change equals time equals impermanence. Nothing is as it ever was. The valve he holds in his hand—solid, heavy, thick—even as he holds it, it is decaying. We cannot experience this, so we imagine having things that are permanent, owning them, expecting them to continue working. His relationship with Laura has dissolved into practically nothing. It will end one day, if it hasn't already this morning, when

151

he dies, or she dies, or he goes away. Nothing is as it ever was—this is what we cannot abide.

"Thanks Tris, you saved my job. It's working
                                                           perfectly, blessed
altar dawning clear upon the light imperial. Vast and wide and going on in all directions dawns a brilliant light. But not a light, a vast clear nothing, more clear than the sun mirrored in the sky upon itself, refracting all beams myriad. I glimpse this searing light for an instant. I see for a moment and understand that I am One with this, and this is God.

Within, without, with calm majestic voice of all the angels sounding every tone at once, a noise magnetic lifts vibration through each particle of light and sound all boiling one the same. A billion suns compressed into one orifice of sound, it commences hot and touches me, a single crashing oneness. Searing open, naked as the sky devours a wisp of cloud: and I am gone. I am nothing now, not even face or hair or nails, nor anger, fear, desire. I am swallowed up by nothing, and every soft explosion centers on my heart, which is now mirror-smooth, splicing each and every part of me within its infinite expanse.

So turn away now, turn away. If I am One with this all-encompassing One, then I will never be my separate self again, I will never touch the cool and lovely night. And so I turn from such a brilliant nothing, for fear of never being me again, for fear of never having darkness by my side.

The names of all the angels reappear, the inward turning reveals to me the forms of all their faces. They rearrange themselves before the split of perfect ripeness, before the boiling sun. I turn into a painful lovely room, an overheated vestibule of shadow, which is the world I know and adore. This darkness carves away a lie, a preposterous offense. Still, it is less fearful than the perfect face of God to turn away to blackness for one instant, so I am knocked

out of here. Come with me. You don't need to stay."

"But, I can't," she says, gripping the railing of the bed and holding on. "They told me I have to stay at least another day or two. They're going to run more tests."

"You don't need to stay. You can come with me."

He holds her other hand, the one that is free. He is not forcibly pulling her out of the bed; neither is he letting go. He is telling her more with the pressure of his closed fist that surrounds her weak free hand that it is time to go with him, it is time to touch him once again.

"Rick," she says, testing. As if saying his name aloud will tell her what the right thing is to do. Holly lifts her head from the pillow to see him more clearly. The room is much the same. The poster of THE AMAZING BACK still there, its strange bony tree trunk filled with nerves. Television going. Bag of fluid still injected in her arm, the arm whose wrist is still bandaged and whose hand still grips the railing. The rolling table with styrofoam cups and a plastic pitcher of melted icewater.

"Where are the kids?"

"With Tom." Her voice snags when she says this other name. "He was kind enough to watch them. I couldn't leave them with my mother."

And something else she notices for the very first time, sitting on the windowsill that runs along one side of the room. A model of what looks like two different types of sponges. One of the sponges is dense, a cross-section propagated with holes of various shapes and sizes. The second sponge is ethereal and light, with large gaps of air between the filaments of substance that make it up. On the base of the model, she reads the word that tells her what this is: OSTEOPOROSIS. She feels her head swim, her breathing go ragged. She wants to sink into unconsciousness again.

"Then you can

come oblivion in a flood of light. I turned away from the face of God, and now I see these eyes that spin forth rays and spears of light. I recommence in moonlight silver, opaline, and furious. I see shimmerings of rose and backwards scoops of glass as intricate as miracles of held taut pearl.

These are my thoughts, the spontaneous presence of my mind. And now I see that my thoughts are things, existing in and of themselves. My mind creates them and sends them into the world. Each one of them can utterly unleash like certain strange inherent liberating aethers, blue pragmatic as the sea.

Spinning, spinning, they do spin forth their rays and spears of ever-colored light. My mind creates these thoughts and each one is an entity that goes into the world in a spiral motion, spreading aureate and blue. With each thought I unleash in this realm, I am released from the world of doubt and terrible appearances I once knew. I am unbound from the simple constraints of the physical world.

I abruptly glimpse dense liquid mass of suns that could be held within arms' reach apart. These balls of light are floating, gliding, colored orbs like fire balloons, like tinted suns three yards across, sprouting rays and orbiting basilicas of strange revolving madness. This is the nature of my thoughts, the nature of my mind.

But I am not yet ready for this place of pure thought, where everything I think can come true in an instant. Secretly, I call upon the dim blue shade of the sixth hour of darkness, I call for the captivity of every sundered thing, which is the physical world.

Did he not say that anyone who has no regard for his life on earth, but despises it, preserves his life forever and ever? At last I understand what he meant by this. I bequeath the unbelief by two and two, for two is aught the same as zero. It is less fearful than the eyes that spin forth rays and spears of light to turn away to blackness for one instant, to turn away undone

by   her own hand, the straps of the bra hang limp astride her collar bones. She exaggerates this slow, restrained unfurling of her self before him. He leans back on the bed and squints his eyes in the late evening haze, and she watches him who watches her. The bra drops to the floor, released. Holly is nothing but pure form now, nothing but a body to enjoy, a supple sure expanse of feeling, a perfect interface connected to the world. An ache of nameless dilation overwhelms her, emerging from her

heart

the spear of light is terrible, is rushing past, a whisper out of dust, open-mouthed and trellised with desire. Spear of light impeccable, invincible, in vulgate and refinement. Pound out the beating of my heart, sound out the declaration of the drought, of fierce enormous waves of light unfolding.

I see beyond the shimmers of my own small incremental thoughts: a sphere that engulfs the heavens with its wide and varied wonders. I see and understand that this astounding sphere of light, incessantly unfurling, is perfect Wisdom. Wide beyond all seeing sphere, as if a sun crouched down, a piece of wonder on a mountainside, deep-sunken and enormous, it bears its weight, its freckled, huge, illuminating weight upon the waves of matchless fivefold light.

But I turn away from this lustrous wide beyond all seeing sphere, I turn away from the open doors of heaven. I am not yet wise enough to be as one with this. If I could bring myself to look upon this glory and give myself up to it, what a heaven I could find. Yet I turn away, for fear of never seeing, never being, never howling into anyone

again he notes upon returning from the errands he has run to waste the waning pale remainder of the weekend that she has left every single blessed light in the house on, the upstairs hallway light, the several master bedroom and bathroom lights, the lights in the master bedroom closet, the lights in two of the three unused bedrooms of this wonderful house they will soon abandon, not to mention several of the lights downstairs, the two old matching lamps in the living room handed down from Tris's grandparents on his mother's side, the half-dozen recessed jar lights with dimmers he installed in the kitchen are on full glare. Even the garish chandelier that looms high above the two-story front foyer is blazing, the one they only use when entertaining party guests. The house is lit like a sinking ocean liner, in the precarious moment before it tips and plunges to its watery grave. And she is nowhere to be found.

He calls to her. His voice rings out and echoes in the towering spaces of the front hallway. "Laura?"

She is not home. She turns the thermostat down to sixty-nine and complains to him about the four hundred dollar electric bill, then leaves the house with every single light on. Not only is she obstinate, she is dumb.

He turns and charges towards the kitchen with the purposeful intent of one who has been wronged. He must turn off all the lights—again. And as he passes through the short corridor that leads to the rear of the house he instinctively glances to his right to catch his reflection in the hallway mirror; but the mirror is gone. She has removed it, along with the photographs of their children and grandchildren that used to hang upon this wall. Packed away—decluttered, no doubt. She has probably gone to take more boxes to the storage unit and the secondhand store. Soon, everything will be gone. Every single thing he has loved in this house, every totem of his life here, packed away and gone. Soon, everything all at once, every single thing that ever was, and ever is, and ever shall be, all at once. It all comes crashing through me, the wayward Babel-din of hearing all the words that ever have been spoken. I see at once all everything before and here and after, spanning limitless illusion, which is the Day of Reckoning.

In every corner sight unbinds me. Every touch sensation ever felt by me or any other, every voice I heard, and all the multitude of waters. I can see every daughter, uncle, baron, king. Each midnight father, every drop of rain and sheaf of wheat. I hear all dimly spoken tongues of long ago and now and ever after. All honey and nectar, and every baby's shriek unanswered.

All orchards, bark of trees, all sparks of life and colonies, all human beings with their burdens. All host of heavens rolled together as a scroll and every human frailty. I hear all hammering, wretched hollering, all touch of sunshine harlequined and every feeling unprocured.

I see and know all kindness, any witness to the angels' matted wings, and every one I reproached and blasphemed. Any first and second fingers, any blemishes or swarms of smoke, all squabbling and discord, any rattling and any tastes that forge from heel of tongue to tip.

All expressions and damnations I ever saw or knew or felt, from whatever lands they hail, all music strange and misery. All weather in succession, every usury and increase. Every homage to betrothed. Yes, I see this is the Day of Judgement, when all will be revealed.

All salt smell, all varnished wood, all hot milk buckets brandished in the cold of dawn. All abominations unto law, and every ooze of life's first rendering.

All half-heard cries of loathing, any ridges, any roots, all wings stretched up unto the sky. All woodlands sweet stillness. I hear and see and taste these things.

This is the sphere of mind unleashed, all ripped into knowing all at once, which is the Day of Judgement. A life I once lived came forth a thousand years ago as if it were one instant. It is a treasure for me to see these scattered fragment lives of mine, impervious to time. They reveal themselves: A desert priest from tribe unknown, an avenger and a slayer. My own mouth battling, the putting out of eyes. The lives reveal themselves: I am a martyr undefiled, a victim of monstrous hammers.

I was once a slave on boarded ships, I was a loping slow apprentice smith. And once I was a child undone by tyranny of parents. I am now a female, now a male. The dead of all the dead and all the living yet to come live on and die with me today. And now the person I have become is shown to me: this is the Day of Reckoning.

Reveal how once I shuffled through a downtown crowd of shoppers, eight years old, my hand in Elmer's hand. Reveal that Elmer feared for me within the landscape of faces all unknown, feared he would lose my hand and lose my little soul, and all the while it was the far distant happiest moment of my life.

Reveal all premonition, all shame and futile regret. The biggest things and every detail of the smallest all at once. Show me how every thing affects another, how it teaches all at once from every person's thoughts, from every person's humiliation.

Show me how many days and people I have known and how they knew me, by what means. We were connected and even still reveal their wondrous names and all their wishes. Each and every stranger gathered together as one with me through nothing but a glance, our eyes and souls connected. I know and comprehend that every accusation, every clattering predicament, each temptation was a reference to my waking Spirit and my waking Soul.

Now reveal a summer's day when I was twenty-three. My life was far diluted, taken up by radio music and TV shows in black and white, and ballgames Elmer listened to, evenings on the porch. One summer's day a man called on me, phantom image of a man from the office where I worked, who from my dreadful diffidence I forgot. He rings the bell and looks through the venetian blinds that cover the front door. He hopes I answer, he wants to see me to the show. His heart is filled with slow degrees of pain and longing for me, for my body youthful and diaphanous. Still young, it looks so young, dear God, and beautiful, yet I coveted and held it back.

I saw the man from behind the shades and cowered there, resisted. I was ever hollow from lack. I turned away; I kept my vigilance to sacrifice. I turned away and never went to answer the door, and in his disappointment he also turned away and never did return.

I lost through arrogance and spite and shame, reveal it all at once, everything I lost. A courtship with this man, and an infant never born. Not one, but two that never came. Show me a life with them that never was, with children of my own, a house in a city far away. A life that is not, was, but could have been. Reveal it as a mirror humiliation, destitute. Show me each moment I was vain, and coarse, and callous, and insane. Show me all the ramifying consequence of each and every word, and act, and thought.

Now I hear a cruel word indeliberate but cunning cruel all the same. A night in spring when Dennis was but ten, he came to me and wanted something quite uneventful, insignificant. Only ten he was, dear Lord, how sweet, how beautiful, how wonderful a boy of ten can be. He wanted but for me to walk him to the store for an evening treat, an ice cream cone or candy. Here reveal each consequence, each ramifying judgement on my soul. I say to him in my distraction, irritation, finishing the crossword puzzle: "NO." The word rings out, and in my anger, for I had had a tiring, difficult day at work, "Get up to your room now and leave me alone."

Alone I am and ever shall be, dear God. It was not much, but now I see it set an ounce of hardness in his heart, it put in place an inch more distance there between us. He turned away in disappointment. He turned away, and I turned back to what, to something tossed away and gone, some thing. No thing should ever supersede another person.

And in eight short years, in less than that, he was gone for good. A moment there I squandered. There are not many moments in a life, a life is here and gone, and those moments when we are young and with our young are of most consequence.

161

I had my pleasures, yes, and underneath all this a second mind revealed, the mind of sleep, of night, of consciousness absconding, all tangled up with every thought that dwells within is outside now. All those underneath and age-old awkward human longings are the halo of my Soul, blown up and out into atonement. It is the day, the hour, when all is monolithic, anonymous, laid bare. There is no hiding, no garnishing, no explaining left to do, all is here laid bare. All thoughts both strident known, unknown, despised. All come to fore, all explode before me here.

The halo of my Soul expands and comes before my judgement. Did I waste the seconds that make up the hours? Did I turn away from mercy? Did I vainly wince and sunken down go feeble, did I shrink away from my talents? Did I perpetuate the race? Did I hold to books instead of friendships? Did I leave my fading hopes untendered from my ancient Soul? Both yes and no.

A fierce unbending light pours forth from me, from the portion that is nothing but a sleepless, commanding eye: This judging, analyzing part of me is my Spirit. This judgement is atoning for the waste, a glare of light that shines unmindful, ever watchful and commanding.

And what is judged, the halo of my all, my deep-known, sleep-known self: This is my Soul.

They watch each other here at last, my Spirit and my Soul. They entertain one last enduring mystery here. They assemble one last time for fullness, soothing happiness, a bursting cycle of voluble connection. My Soul, untendered, is joined unto my

Spirit, to the glare of light that shines unmindful, ever watchful. One judgement more, one final deep abomination, one burning, glamorous candidate for a deep and

heavy headache, Holly sits up in bed and looks for something to drink. There is a glass of old water from the night before or maybe several days ago, before she went into the hospital. She takes it up and drinks from it, a sip and then a gulp. And she turns to find that he is still there, rolled up in a ball with his back turned away, his enduring perfectly socketed back. The amazing back. What is she to do with him now that it is Monday and she is home and her girls are not home, they are in the home of another man while this man is here with her. At least it is Monday, she is not missing any more work. She stares at the bandage on her wrist; a spot of brown where the blood wore through, it needs to be changed. Could she take it off and go to work tomorrow? Or maybe wear a long-sleeved blouse, something light enough to be comfortable even in the August heat.

The air conditioning kicks in, the rising air slashing at the window blinds gives her a chill and she recoils into the blankets once again, nudging him awake. Scent of sleeping bodies washing over her, scent of sex. He grumbles and rolls over, eyes still shut against the noonday light. Reaching out, his arms instinctively intertwine with hers and they collapse into clinging misalignment. His hardness is reassuring. He is always hard, every part of him. His free top hand explores her lower back and the slight paired indentations where the cleft between her buttocks begins. This could be good, having him here in the morning for

163

a change, first time this has ever happened. She allows herself to be drawn in closer, pressing her breasts against him, this is the only family she has today. Her head feels as if a sea of black smooth oil is washing against the walls of her skull, a neutral pounding with every movement. She could make him stop and bring her some aspirin. But he never stops, he never wants to stop.

"I bet that limp-wrist Tom doesn't give it to you like this."

The whispered words come to her confused, far away, muffled by a layer of her own fine hair and the pliable mass of the pillow. He would be perfect, the perfect man, if he never opened his mouth. If only he would keep his mouth shut, she could keep him around for a while.

She pulls her head away from him and looks at his face. Long nose, thin and aquiline. Dark eyebrows nearly grown together above it. Mouth and lips that know how to make her move. Hair close-cropped stubble receding from the brow. And eyes that look back to her with challenging half-masked fear and derision. He has been as beaten-down by life as she has, she can see that in his eyes.

"You want him, go ahead. Just because he buys you things, rides you around in his car."

Why is he saying these things, why now? He must know her better than she realizes. His understanding is pure animal and instinctual, conveyed by sense of touch, from his hands and arms and thighs locked around her. He must have felt that she was missing Zoe and Jenny.

"What are you talking about? I never said anything about him."

"Yes you did. At the hospital. Telling me that he is taking care of your girls, your precious girls. So what?" His eyes plunge into floating broken anger. "You never even let me see them—not once."

Again she considers how his absolute animal knowledge has drilled straight to the heart of the issue, to an understanding subliminal and dispersed. She has not consciously kept the girls from him, but now that he has said this, she realizes that she has until now never let him set foot in her apartment, and perhaps he has seen the reason all too clearly.

"That's not true, you could see them if you want." She has to tread carefully around the variations that could arise from this. It could go any number of ways. "It's just that . . . we always meet late, after work. The kids are home asleep or at the sitter's house."

"Why wouldn't you want me to see them? Here you are living in this two-bedroom dump of a place, cutting hair for a living, your head so screwed up you don't even mind if I crack it in two, and yet . . . " He gropes for a word; he isn't used to making such a lengthy speech. "The only one good enough to see your precious darlings is limp-wrist Tom. You had it all planned out, didn't you?"

"What are you talking about? It wasn't my choice to end up in the hospital and have him come charging over to save me."

"Sure it was. Everything is your choice." He removes his arm from under her waist and sits up in the bed. "Listen Holly.

I need a place to stay, for a few days at least. My landlord, they kicked me out. Too many rubber checks."

So that's it. No wonder he didn't want to go to his place. Her mind calculating precisely the next actions that must be taken, the ramifications of her very next words. She envisions him waking up here in bed with her day after day, a strange man in the house when the girls go to the kitchen for their cereal. No, he cannot stay here, this place is for her and for her girls, he must

go with a cataclysm that ripped the earth and sky completely apart. My Soul and my Spirit ripped in two, the reflection of me undone. My Spirit sees and understands what is happening in a cold, analytical way. My Soul stumbles along in a trance of wonder, circling round about itself. My Spirit is the light that shines inside, pure consciousness, forever watching whatever comes its way; and my Soul records every single thing the Spirit hears and sees and feels, faithfully balling it up into a proud and hopeful, scared and dream-distorted memory. And now, these two parts of me are ripped apart.

Spirit sees what the Soul can no longer register: After about forty-eight hours of no blood to the corpus collossum—the short, leathery band of tissue connecting the two hemispheres of the brain—it no longer provides the Soul and Spirit with the interface they shared in the physical world. The final tenuous link to the body is broken, and so, the majestic mind of Amelia Geist is torn in two. This is the Second Death.

Spirit stares immaculate, unmindful, stares and watches the veil of blackness descend. There is no here, no anywhere but outsetting vastness encompassed all in darkness. Spirit watches and stares, alone. Amazed in silent ancient fear, dead stars are ripped apart. Two things that always worked together, that must behave as one, are ripped apart. Folds of leather tissue in the skull go dry and fall apart. The tomb in Palestine stands empty, thrown open to a world where earth and sky rebuke each other. Their postures echo and resound with the final crack of heaven splitting in a dream.

Spirit is pure consciousness, immaculate and empty. It sees that Amelia's Soul is holding fast to the life it left behind. Amelia's Soul is stuck in the world, still clinging to the things it loves and hopes for. The Soul is pure feeling, it cannot analyze what has happened to it and understand. It cannot comprehend that Amelia is no longer alive, because to this dreamlike sphere of pure emotion, Amelia and everything that made her up is all there ever was and ever is. It lingers there, clutching the earth and all its pleasures, doubts, and fears. And if it does not let go, it will remain there—stuck, a forlorn and haunting presence, another broken fragment of life that Spirit left behind.

Spirit has an impulse to reach out, to bring Amelia's Soul back and make itself whole again. But nothing moves here, no thing unfolds, there is no temperature to comfort. There is no time, no moment after moment, there is only Spirit, unbounded and everlasting, who watches and stares, and

in another place there is also my Soul, my deep-known, sleep-known self, still wondering about me, still circled back upon the me that ever was and has been.

My garden awaits. Here all places are as one, so here is my garden, flowers draping over me, tender fronds of snaps. The stalks and stems lift all about me. Here is dirt still damp and wet. Red dusk globes of cone flowers, tender fronds of snaps on gabbling stalks surround me, luminous lavender and bronze. Here is my garden, my plot of earth, my pinoak great observant.

Inside my home, the dining room has my breakfront with my pictures, plates, and keepsakes still inside. These are plates we ate on thirty, forty years ago, Elmer, Father, and Louise, Karl and me and Dennis. The porcelain vase is gone, but where is it? The porcelain vase is gone.

In the living room, I brush past the frayed and weathered chair where I sit and watch the shows here by the window. And Enrique on the porch, on his metal chair he watches the street with the chain-link fence in front. I touch his shoulder, his wrinkled shirt, to let him know I am here. He doesn't see me— he does not feel.

Enrique looks to the yard and the street, but not to me. My words come out, but he does not hear. He hears instead the telephone ring inside his house. He gets up and turns past me, not seeing, opens the door and goes inside. The phone

keeps

ringing, and Holly sits up in bed to answer it, and he is still here. She answers the phone cradling the receiver between her chin and shoulder as she reaches for a cigarette.

"Yes?"

"Is this Holly Schenk?"

"Who's calling?"

"This is McEnbreit and Flannerty mortuary. Am I speaking to Holly Schenk?"

"Yes. What is this . . . regarding?" She lights the cigarette and brings it to her lips. "I'm not interested, whatever you're selling."

"No ma'am. We're not selling. We were given your name as a hairdresser to style the hair of a deceased person in preparation for final viewing—by special request."

"Whose request?"

"Request of the deceased. We sometimes get a request for a favorite hairdresser to style a person's hair. In this case, Amelia Geist informed us, as it turns out, the day before she passed away."

"What on earth are you talking about? I'm not going to... "

But then she looks at him lying there in bed, his dark eyes hooded, thick, staring at her, and sees she has an excuse to leave. She wasn't expecting to leave him today, but she has always known how to push someone away when they get too close to her—even her own girls at times, when they demand too much, especially Zoe, who sometimes clings and needs more attention. When she feels oppressed by them she must escape. She deposits the burning cigarette in the ceramic art class whale Zoe made at school, which serves as a makeshift ashtray on the bedside table. For an instant Holly wonders: Do whales have teeth? Zoe's thumbprints are clearly visible around the mouth hole, each separate impression of the thumb designed to provide the whale a tooth.

Holly's underwear and bra are on the floor where she dropped them. A floral-pattern blouse and jeans are there too—the clothes she was wearing when she entered the hospital, the ones she wore when she left, one sleeve of the blouse still spattered with blood. They will have to do. Pulling the jeans on, she sees that Rick was ahead of her in his understanding. Having him here in the apartment, in her own bed, was going too far. Rick had been a means of escape for her, but having him here in her own bed, making demands, has transformed him into another obligation, another trap to hold her. And she also senses that she has finally found her own level: Whereas Tom was too good for her, this man is not good enough.

"What are you doing?"

She hesitates as her mind constructs an answer. The words that come out surprise her. "I'm going to help a friend."

"Get your ass back in bed." He is up quickly. He is taller than she is, his physical presence is intimidating; but the most shocking thing about him, the thing that might make her stay, is his eyes. They look at her in disbelief, like the eyes of a dog that has been left at the side of the road by its owner.

She turns towards the door, and his hand is on her in an instant. He is holding onto her wrist hard enough to hurt, squeezing as if he wants to crush the blood out of her. But this grip he has on her flayed and bandaged wrist is the last time he will ever touch her, and he must know it. He has overstepped the boundary.

"It's time to let me

go to Louise's house. Her house is as it was and ever shall be. Here the cupboards overlook the sink, the kitchen window, and all is buffeted by shadows creeping from the trees. It is summer still, it is still a hot and hangworn day outside, with branches full of leaves that overlook the steep and shaded hill with the creek far below in the distance, beautiful to see.

Louise has lived in Bremerton since she was gone and off to college, first college girl in the family, and never let us forget it. When she came home from school for Christmas break, her forehead high as her bosom, she was always reading books and studying for the next exam and writing papers. All she did was read and write and talk of what she would do after college, after graduate school. She was going to be what none of us could be, she was always smarter than the rest. But here she is, still in Bremerton, still stuck in the woods with her books.

This hallway leads to bedrooms and a bath. It is a cottage in the woods, dark-lit, only shadows from the noonday trees here tower over, block the sun. The bathroom has a sink, a vanity with her things, her lotions, soap, and towels. What does water feel like? Warm and slippery, a tub, a sink; the tap is open, water, warm and slippery. Threadbare towels, all things are worn, all here and now is worn and wrought of simpler stuff, and still to me is lovely.

This bed between a closet and a wall is cosseted with full and faded ripeness. The wood floors are bare except for a rug curled up at one end from being kicked and tripped on many times. Her feet have done this, tripped it into a curl. The table by the bed is stacked with books. She reads, and on the floor-boards in the corner by the closet more haphazard stacks of books. The closet smells of must, of clothes she seldom wears. A pair of dungarees lies wadded on the floor. To me this smell is wonderful, this scent of gingham, scent of trees she brought in from the hill.

Each of these things are wonderful, are gorgeous, are all the same as me, and part of me. She keeps her time in one main room where her favorite chair is, her favorite place to read. In all the years she watches her figure still, her bosom sets up high. And yes, of course, she is reading, always reading. What do all the books tell her? How many words has she taken in, how many thoughts and phrases, and look where it has gotten her: Still here in the woods outside of Bremerton, all alone as me. And yet it is Louise, my betrayer and also now a comfort, both of these combining on her body. I would like to bring forth repentance on her body, frail and withered, because her body is now an object to gratify the waves of my remembering, the memories of the children we were still clinging here and set to cry.

I reach out to touch this frail and withered person, and as I do it Father screamed, in memory. Suddenly, I see what book she reads, and the stream of what she's feeling overflows within me, as I touch her massy shoulder, her hair exhausted, betrayer of me. She feels the murk of long neglect, anxiety for what the future holds. She does not look, or move, or talk. She reads the words again *succeeds to night,* and across the room the fireplace doors are a black reflecting glass. Louise, restricted in her chair, book in hand, head bent to read, as ever she was and has been. And by her side where the image of me in the black fireplace glass should be, there is nothing. There is no me any longer, no me in body, form, or

person opens the door to the bright room chilled by air conditioning and a waft of chemical smell overwhelms her. It is as if she has returned to the hospital again, the antiseptic determination of activity about the body, the shining stainless steel equipment gleaming with its promise of purity and health. But here she is a visitor—no, even more, she is one of the workers. And the body they are attending to lies on a steel table, cold, the sight of the bare purple soles of the old woman's feet at the end of the table, toes pointing outward in a horizontal *plié,* confirms it: Holly is no longer the patient.

"You may go ahead." The woman who has led Holly to the cloistered room and opened the door for her indicates with a stern flat hand a lab table on which various hair cutting and styling tools have been set out. "The decedent made a simple request—to have you duplicate the style you gave her before."

Holly sees the body lying flat on the metal table, plain white sheet covering most of the naked torso, and cannot conceive of touching it.

"Shouldn't be hard. I just cut her hair on Friday."

The woman nods. She is accustomed to the monotony of death. One more body on the table, receiving the same treatment. Holly has a sudden panic: What if the woman leaves her here

173

alone with me, with my body. This body on the table is mine alone, and yet they watch it, shrouded, naked, and cold, with garments unsewn. This body is mine alone to know. No other hand should touch it, no other eyes should see.

The reason why I cannot leave is here beneath me, my cold and naked body, shrouded, all alone. The problem is, I believed in my own suffering, I bereaved my unwanted solemn flesh. I believed that my body was my self, that there is no other temple, and so it will always be. I spend this gazing moment imagining what never now could happen: Bring forth rapport, bring to me my body my own, to house my Soul profuse and dissipate, as though nothing here on earth collapses.

And all the while I am barred from my body. In my impotence I stand alone in terror, and thus remain astonished. They wait and watch and pray, or no, they touch things aside at the table. They talk about my self, defile and transgress. They do not pray, they prepare to

touch the hair for the first time, and it is only hair. Holly has to remind herself that this is only hair like all the other hair she touches every day, dead as soon as she cuts it and lets it fall to the floor. All the hair she touches, all the heads she touches, are the same as this, only this one does not move or talk to her. There is nothing inside—that's the only difference. That, and the eyes are closed. They have placed caps on top of the eyes, the eyelids, to cover them, perhaps to keep them shut. She wants to ask the woman about them—these caps are not natural, they keep the eyes closed. But they are better than having the eyes open, staring up at her. The caps are not good, but Holly cannot imagine having the eyes staring up at her, wide open but unseeing, open but not watching while she does this work. There is only misperception here. A body that no longer works, lying down but no longer at rest. That is what Holly cannot get out of her head as she rinses the hair out and prepares to wash it. This was a person two days ago, who watched her children, who lived and breathed and laughed and gave the girls candy, and brought somehow the shadow of death among them.

The hair is tangled. Holly applies a conditioner to it, working it into the sheaths of longer hair at the back to disengage the follicles. Of course it's tangled. The hair hasn't been washed for several days and has endured whatever illness or trauma led to dying. And then being transported here and lying crushed under the weight of the head for days in which they have done whatever it is they do to a body to keep it from disintegrating. The face is surprisingly supple. The area around the eye sockets has sunken down a bit and the lips are pressed together, taut, but otherwise she might only be asleep. The hair is lathered now and slick, and the action of Holly's hands makes it feel warmer. Motion, motion is life. So she keeps her hands moving, working the hair into smooth dark strands exposed beneath the

touch of
when shame and reproach would whisper my dismissal, and all the many reasons not to touch rolling through me only kept my wrapped and vanquished body forcefully faltered from explore. I have had a slatted wisdom, a woven tapestry of substitute despair. This helper comes to touch the body I lost, and lovers are

only destroyed by shame and reproach. This helper squeezes my hair in ceremony, squeezes tighter and lets go, working only as much as required to prepare for the final day when my body belongs to the earth.

But it has always been so. It has always been vanity that kept me wrapped and vanquished, bound up in unworthiness, and look at it now, the lips that never touched another, the hands that never held. Look at it under this sheet, a whole breadth of kneaded flesh unused and covered in a veil, unwanted, unentered, never listened to nor held. Kneel and pray and never know a clashing wrong, not vulgar, not if it was a part of me, my body. How could it be otherwise, surrounded by life and suddenly destroyed by shame and reproach. This helper will like the others not hesitate to touch or hide her

quick motions, direct and to the point will get it done. There is no need to cut; that was done the other day. So the style should hold nicely. The woman says it is helpful to fasten the hair with bobby pins along the sides where the head will be lying in the casket, in order to keep the hair in place, as the body is removed and placed in the box. How did she say it? As the body is casketed.

Don't think about it. In a box lying there in one position forever, for a very long time at least, until whatever it is that eats the body . . . don't think about it. And then only bones remain. Comb it forward into a series of layered curls tight around the temples, cheeks, and forehead. Those dim, dark circles she was sinking into, this woman has already gone there. It could have been Holly, could have very easily been Holly here on the table, circles of darkness each one wider than the one before. In back, the head must be lifted up—this is not easy—in order to comb out and set. The head seems heavy as a bowling ball, putting one hand underneath to lift gently, then comb, and the woman shakes her head from across the room, saying not to worry about that part, it will not be on display in the casket.

Lay the head down gently and comb. The hair is drying now, a little more brittle than usual, but still easy to work with. Comb forward, comb into tight curls around the temples and forehead. No blowdrying according to the woman, which makes it a little more difficult to texture the style. This styling will be viewed only once, by only a few people, unlike the thousands of other cuts and styles she has given over the years that are seen day in and day out for a period of weeks, but this style perhaps is the most important of all, a final lasting image for those who have known this woman throughout her long life. And because it will provide the final image, it must look as much alike the living woman as possible, this woman who failed Holly, who let the one who has fractured her into the house with her daughters. And yet, how could she have known? How could anyone have known? Holly didn't, at first. And neither did the others. So how could this woman, unless Holly told her; and she didn't. So the one who fractured all the lives went into the house and broke open another. But the life he touched and broke open is only the life of the body, only the part of her that will one day lie on a cold metal table like this with only a thin sheet to cover her, and that part of her will shrink and dissipate and turn cold as the table, so how could Holly all these years let him ruin all the other parts that want to live and breathe forever?

A glance from the woman tells Holly it is time to finish—perhaps there is another body that will soon come to the room and be injected with chemicals. Combing a few more thin strands of hair onto the forehead in a scalloped row of bangs, Holly notices now that the pads of fat around the armpits have shrunk; how she can tell this is impossible to know. But it is true, they look shriveled, less full somehow. All the body, the upper torso around the shoulders she can see above the crisp line of sheet, appears to have shrunk. Perhaps it is because the fat, the cells have lost water, all the water in us that keeps us supple and

smooth and lonesome impulse. The hand is a revelation, hand and arm and face closed up, retreated, startling they are still here by themselves, without me. Bring forth to me my body once again, my self is only mine to know. Bring forth to me my hand, my face. Bring to me my arms, my legs, my shoulders bare and cold, my face closed up, retreated. I want to be inside my self again, to go inside the veins, and arteries, and lungs. To go within my heart, to inhabit all the parts of me, to move again, to sweat and breathe and feel the flesh go quick within the

movement happens so quickly Holly cannot be quite sure she saw it. But she did see it. The body moved, the arm twitched somehow and the hand jerked up off the table, and it startles her so that she backs away a step and drops the comb she had been holding. "My God," she says across the room to the woman, "did you see that?"

"See what?"

"It moved. The body moved."

The woman comes closer now, not so much to see anything but to be near Holly. She stands beside Holly and is as calm and bored as ever.

"Well, it may have. It happens sometimes. The chemicals we use for embalming will sometimes constrict the muscles as they soak into the tissue, and that can cause an involuntary movement. Just a twitch."

Holly knows she saw it move, and now she only wants to get out of this room, get out of here as quickly as possible. The woman looks at her and puts a hand on her arm.

"It's okay, I understand how this can be startling."

Holly doesn't answer. She takes one last look at the sheet-shrouded body and

follows a river that flows from one place to forever. Spirit is pure consciousness; Spirit is the everlasting I. The suitable and single I of the Spirit can see and hear more now than I can ever know. I can see the white ascending river that flows from one place to forever, which is the White Abyss.

How can I be one and two and more than that alone? Yet, I can. I flow into the world of perfect forms, by simply seeing it. I embroider all the wreathed and savoured offerings unto every Spirit wild with life that flows here. Many forms and many Spirits move here, all of them borne on a rushing current of white energy from one life to the next. This river is a passage, a way station, a place where I can seek and find the perfect form in which to live again. This is nothing but a river that rushes through every Spirit with the noble hope of ascending towards another life again.

And yet. I know there is a part of me I left behind, a broken piece of me that lingers on the earth, along with all the other parts of me that did not find their way to Heaven. It suffers still, like all the others. It bundles up and lives again the hopes and fears that were not mastered. It suffers all the unmet longings, all the forlorn passions and potentials that were never found, or were forgotten. But another life is calling. I deliver every crowded willing pleasure. I see more now than ever.

And through the moonlight strangeness of this realm, I enunciate the feverish serving hand. I dictate the fierceness of the offerings, the washed expectant runners through the land, crossing the White Abyss, this tumbling, rushing water, firm with purpose, flush with life. I see alone the perfect ways of all the watching secret

            things have always been hard to understand, and so they simply have to be obeyed. Certain impulses must be followed, no matter where they might lead. Holly has found herself at the doorstep of the old woman's house with no good reason to be here and no reason to knock; nobody lives here anymore.

The door is unlocked, so she enters. The living room is undisturbed, the late afternoon sun filtering through venetian blinds that clink together as she closes the door behind her. Stillness and quiet surround her. Not even the ticking of a clock to mar the settled air within this room. Has anyone been here since? There is no sign. The half-eaten bag of chips, the empty soda cans, the recliner still launched at an angle for watching the television, aimed at the box. Why hasn't anyone come to clean? In this dim and settled space she feels as if she is the only one who has ever been here, totally alone.

She looks around and tries to find something to tell her why it happened, where. She has only a hazy vision of what must have taken place, formed mainly from her own recollections, images blazoned upon her heart from moments in her own childhood, long ago. The old woman's things, in the daily disarray of a life arrested in mid

motion here in my home, here she is again, the one who touched my body and would not let me enter. Here she moves about and motions in my home, she moves about and steps within it. She comes to look at me and now at my things, my home. She comes to touch. But I will not let her. If she would not let me go into my body, I will not let her enter my home. I will push her away, and more than that. I will put my hands on her neck and strangle her. I will grab her by her face and push her out the door. All the ones I wanted to come back never did

come back to her with all the feelings that can get locked up in things. What is it she wants to find here? She has a prickling of the skin at the back of her neck, crawling up from her shoulders, a feeling that someone else is with her. A brief puff of air brushes against her cheek, as if someone has expelled a silent, malevolent syllable towards her ear. Holly glances over her shoulder and turns around to see that no one is here. The room is quiet and still as ever. The fine blond hair on her forearms stands on end, gooseflesh rising on her legs. But she has the fragment of porcelain in her hand, and she knows now what to do with it.

She steps across the room and sees a mark on the wall above the sofa, a chip in the wainscotting. And beneath the mark, on the shoulder of the couch, are chips of porcelain, white dust that shows her this is where it happened, where the pitcher broke.

The porcelain stained with her own blood is cool in her hand. She grips it tightly for a moment, holding on to it like a child that clutches a coin, then lets go, allowing it to fall to the floor. She turns and strides toward the door, grasping the doorknob. But even as she's pushing her way out of the house, an object catches her eye, a brightly colored pamphlet on the tottering oval table next to the recliner:

HORACE MANN HIGH SCHOOL

CLASS OF 1957

REUNION

Holly remembers now—this is why the old woman wanted to have her hair done, for the reunion. This is not a pamphlet, it looks like pages printed out from a computer, stapled together. And at the bottom of the first page, she sees something scrawled in pencil, in the old lady's spidery script, a name and a phone number:

Tris 415-555-3462

Maybe someone she knew. Holly smiles to think of it—even an overweight, lonely old woman like that primping and having her hair done as if she were a teenager going to the prom. To think of someone with skin as fine and parchmentlike as that old woman's wanting to see a man, some old codger she knew a hundred years ago, in another life. She wants to hurry out of the house; that puff of breath on her cheek, like death itself brushing against her. But she has let go of one thing and along comes another, the pull of another person always approaching with the promise of acceptance and a place on this earth she can safely call her own. As she shuts the door behind her, she fishes for the cell phone in her purse and dials the number on the paper, an area code she doesn't know, and reaches out for another connection

to the earth and all its wonders is too strong in me, all the parts of me I cling to as a consolation are here and with me still, but just beyond my reach. I am in my house but not a part of it. I can see my body, but I am no longer in it. I can see these people, the woman who touched me and Louise, but I cannot even talk to them. I reach out to touch and they do not feel or hear or see. And here the darkness creeps across the floor, a dusk that settles like a layer of silt on the furniture and dims each edge and corner. Darkness is a lack, and I have found that even a lack is something too, an absence of anything or any one that can grow until it overwhelms all other things. Darkness is the absence of light, a lack that grows and grows.

Here all places are as one and all times. The clock that juts from the corner of the department store is stuck, its hands are frozen at 9:27, and no one can say whether this is morning or evening, or when the hands decided suddenly to stop. The people glance up at it, but not to check the time. They love to see the green filligree of the arm that extends from the cornice of the building, the copper scrollwork along the top. Their eyes look at me, but do not see. Their mouths move, but no words come out. And always I am waiting. Here I am and always shall be. He said to meet him here at half past two and we will see the matinee; they still charge the early prices for this show. I watch for him to come along in the crowds of shoppers, his face isolated from the rest simply because it is his, well known and loved. But he never does come. He never did love me and never will.

The darkness grows, darkness and cold of night. The sidewalk grows dim and opens onto a broad expanse of space, as broad as the open gulf of sky that used to spread beyond my window when I was a girl and couldn't go to sleep, and watched for shooting stars to fly. But there are no stars here. This is an open field, brown and barren and cold, devoid of trees. The sky is black and the earth crunches under my feet. As I walk, one place becomes another. The downtown street transforms itself into this marshy landscape that stretches in all directions. Each step I take is a step away from the solid, comfortable spaces that contained my past. I reach my arm out and feel currents in the air; perhaps there is another person nearby. I have come to a place it seems where people move together through the gloom, together but apart. And now a voice, disembodied in the blackness, whispers my name:

"Amelia."

Whispered, but calling out distinctly, calling for me to come. I want to turn away from it, but there is only one way to go here—the direction that leads me to the voice and always circles back into myself.

Time is a vapor here. My day is over now and here is my night, unending, everlasting night. I have only just arrived, but I feel as if I have been here forever.

I keep moving forward and hear, in the distance, a child's voice cry out. A presence hovers near, I can feel it; perhaps it is the voice that called me. As one sense goes away, the others become stronger, so I can hear many things more clearly than ever before. The sound of scuffling feet and the grinding of a machine, the wooden, rusty creaking of a mill that takes in something and crushes it. The sounds come to me in pools, like spots of cold stillness in a stream, and I can hear the cry of a child that is pierced through with pain. The child releases another cry

all you want, we are going to this funeral."

Jenny takes over where her younger sister left off. She sees that the little girl tactic of throwing a fit is not working, so she turns to the overbearing logic of the teenager expressing her independence. "Why are you making us *go?*" She takes another stab at it, more forceful, demanding her rightful place in the world, trying a mixture of guilt and sheer stubborn determination. "You can't make us go to this. That old lady was creepy, in her smelly old house. She didn't even really watch us."

185

Holly hears the unstated message from Jenny: now I may use whatever happened there with Steve against you.

"We're going because I said so, and I'm the parent."

"But she's dead, Mom. Who cares? I didn't want to see her before, and I sure don't want to see her now."

With the mention of the fact that the woman is dead, Zoe lets out another cry, a slobbering snuffling noise designed to so irritate and distract Holly that she will give up the fight.

"It's good to see that everything is back to normal." Tom smiles and adjusts the tautness of his suspenders. Only a lawyer who pulls down as much cash as Tom would take this as an opportunity to wear something as ostentatious as this. But he is right. The fact that they are arguing with her is proof enough that Holly's stay in the hospital has not been a major trauma for her daughters, at least on the surface. They are too preoccupied with their own lives. This feels like any of the other workaday mornings when she has to drag the girls away from the television to feed them breakfast and get them ready for school.

"That lady asked me to be there."

"How could she do that? She's dead." For some reason, Jenny likes saying that she's dead. Probably to see if she can scare her sister.

"She did it in her will." This is stretching the truth, but it may reach into the realm of adult legal affairs that are just enough beyond the girl's understanding that she drops her all-knowing teenage attitude. "In her will," Holly says, "she asked me to do her hair when she died, and that means I also have to go to the funeral, to make sure everything looks okay." Holly has to cinch the waist of the dress Tom bought her last night, so she would have something decent to wear to this. Though Tom insisted, she did not want to go back to the apartment, in case Rick were still there. Even so, she did have a feeling that Rick might have already left. "She needs us. Everybody needs people to be with them when they die."

The unexpected ring of truth in Holly's last statement resonates through the two-story entryway of Tom's house and halts, at least for the moment, the unbecoming protests of her girls. She remembers now another way in which she can enforce her will as parent, the action that demonstrates "because I said so" vividly and without question: She turns and leaves the room. End of discussion.

Though she has left the front hallway, Holly is still in the same large cathedral-like space as Tom and the children. The clicking of her heels on the floor echoes as she walks. Tom's house is a vast series of open areas, one leading to another, living room, dining room, great room, kitchen, foyer, and mud room, separated only by varying types of furniture and architectural details such as faux Doric columns, a fireplace, or a line where the plush carpeting ends and a wood or tile floor begins. A soaring staircase leads to the upper floor, which is open to most of the lower level and overlooks it from an elegant white and blonde wood railing. Holly is always amazed by the kitchen. It alone could contain her entire apartment. The pantry is larger than the bedroom where the girls sleep, and has two doors. She examines the extravagant display of pots and pans and utensils, glimmering silver and gold as they hang from hooks in the ceil-

ing high above. It is all shiny and clean, every appliance spar-
kling, immaculate. She can't imagine him using any of this, it
looks as artificial as a Hollywood movie set. It is as if he has
prepared this house for a wife, it is ready and waiting for her—
whoever she may be. She lets her mind wander here: Perhaps it
is meant to be me. She feels the small muscles in her back un-
tense with the thought of settling in to the safety of Tom's
money.

"We should go." Tom has come up behind her and placed
his hand discreetly on her shoulder. He would not touch her
anywhere else. The girls have followed him and sullenly trudge
past to the back hallway that leads to the garage. They know
their way around here. Holly can tell that they have not minded
staying with Tom these past few days. When she arrived here
from the old lady's house, she felt as if she were an outsider, an
unexpected visitor intruding on the makeshift family Tom had
fashioned for himself. And she saw in the eyes of Jenny and
Zoe something broader, less fearful.

There are three cars in the four-car garage, but Tom's blood-
stained BMW is not one of them.

"Let's take the Jeep."

The girls open the back door and scramble in to the olive-
colored car with the open top defined by a cage of tubular black
roll bars. It is a challenge to hoist herself three feet up into the
vehicle without catching her dress on her heels, but once she is
inside, it is as comfortable as any other car she has been in, with
leather seats and a console full of dials and buttons. Tom turns
the ignition and backs out of the garage.

"You got rid of the Beamer?"

Tom's eyes roll up and to the right, as he checks the mirror to turn the car around in the driveway. "I wanted something a little more . . . rugged. I looked at the new Land Rovers, but they felt like I was driving a Cadillac on stilts." And as if to convince himself further that he has made the right decision, he adds, "The girls love it."

"We went for a ride in the country." Zoe's voice still holds the excitement of a child who can be entertained by something more than television shows, pop music, or video games. "We drove over a field with big rocks in it, and the car didn't even tip."

Holly glances at Tom, for an instant questioning his judgment over the past few days as a surrogate father for her girls. She studies his hand as he shifts the car out of reverse. Hairless, smooth, accustomed to manipulating gadgets such as computer keyboards and cell phones and steering wheels with small, precise movements. She remembers something he told her in the hospital as if it might have been a dream, a half-forgotten image from a world far removed and long ago: "Listen Holly, I want to marry you." Not a proposal exactly, more like an opening statement in the kind of lengthy discourse he is accustomed to. The span of time since that moment feels like forever; perhaps he never really said it.

Tom's skin is the color of autumn. She has always thought of him that way. His cheeks are ruddy and flushed, as if he has just come inside from picking apples on a windswept afternoon. Maybe he was out of season when she met him, earlier in the summer. He is comfort and consolation. He is all the things she has fled over the years: thoughtfulness and logic, care and consideration. Having all the things he has—the house, the cars—is only another type of contract with the world, a legal covenant with one person, one place. And perhaps, if it happened, she would become merely another one of his possessions in this house—the final accessory to complement the shiny bright counter tops and appliances in his well-appointed kitchen. As they wind down the driveway towards the road into town, she can see yet another indication of the kind of place this is: Astride the black asphalt, two berms, each of which has been landscaped with a low wall of butter-colored stone and banks of golden flowers that receive the flattering glow of the late morning light. And between the two walls, obstructing the drive, a black wrought-iron gate, no higher than the shoulder of a child.

"Why do you have a gate, when the walls can't keep anyone out?" She has asked him this before, but she tries again, to see if he will give a different answer.

"I like the way it looks." He reaches above his head and presses a button on a small box clipped to the sun visor, like opening a garage door. "I always wanted to drive through a gate when I arrive at my home."

They roll to a stop for a moment, as the gate rises up. Gates can keep people in just as easily as they keep people

out of the rubber flaps that protect the opening from which the conveyor belt emerges, another black suitcase slithers into the world, nearly identical to the rest.

Tris watches one bag push through the flaps and lurch towards him, brown with pink and slate blue circles in a mod sixties op art pattern. Mesmerizing, he stares at it and forgets to look for his own bag. Lack of sleep has put him in a trance. He cannot even believe he is here. The red-eye flight made nightmarish by a woman sitting next to him with the overhead light on all night, filling out page after page of a Japanese puzzle book consisting of grids of numbers. At one point, he asked her what she was doing, and why.

"To pass the time," she said, still scratching in another numeral even as she spoke. "It keeps my mind sharp."

He slumped against the bulkhead by the window and tried to get some sleep. But the sun rolled around and blasted its absurd and sublime light through the cracks around the window shade, and soon the fifty-minute layover in Chicago came, with just enough time to trudge through the never-ending terminal, closing his eyes as he rode the moving sidewalk from one concourse to the next. The twenty minute flight to Middlesborough on a half-empty plane is not even there for him to remember—he must have slept.

Laura is probably sleeping still, in bed without him; she will wonder where he is when she wakes up. He left her a note in the kitchen, but the note is a lie, a vague half-truth about an emergency at the food processing plant in New Jersey. Of course, he will go to New Jersey later on today, but he did not tell her that he is stopping here in Middlesborough first, and it gives him that old feeling again of being in the wrong place; always he is somewhere he should not be. Another black bag comes through the flaps and jolts along the conveyor belt. They travel around in a circular loop as the weary passengers watch them go by, and every now and then a hand reaches down and snatches one of them up. Some of the bags do not get taken; they make the entire circuit and go through another set of flaps into the unseen realm behind the wall. Those bags will come back again on the other side.

Perhaps he should forget the whole thing and go

home is far away from here, and I am far away from him. The machine grinds on, the wooden wheel of the mill is taking people in and grinding the grist with the sickening sound of bones being crushed. Where did the child who was crying go?

Two hands, two arms, come up from behind and wrap themselves around me. The hands are cold, the arms hold tight around my shoulders; turning to see what this is, there is only a current in the night. I try to shrug it away, but it is slippery smooth, like the darkness I walked through when I entered this place. Of course, this is the presence that called to me. It reaches around and tugs at something deep within my chest. In effect, it feels as if I am being turned inside out, as if I have been opened up and something is being torn from me and extracted. I cannot see what this is, in the stifling darkness, but the other senses more than make up for blindness—taste and smell and touch combine into one sensation that works here. The thing that has been ripped from me is a ball of tangled black and red resistance, a wet, acrid taste, a fullness in the mouth, with loose cords of flesh all covered in esters black as tar. It is

192

smaller than a shoebox, bound up like a knot, a spiral core of tight-woven muscle and tendons hanging. It is true, every manner of pain comes from within: I had no regard for my life on earth, yet here I am, encompassed in darkness. All the promises ever made to me have come to nothing. I want to cry out as that child did before, and perhaps I do but cannot hear it, all I hear is the slippery presence whispering my

name in the book where everyone is supposed to sign when they first arrive. The foyer of the funeral home has been appointed with fussy, uncomfortable-looking armless chairs that no one ever sits on. But the room is cheerful enough, the August sun hangs high in the heat of late morning, and every object in the room is pulled into distinct clarity by the abundance of its light. Tom has led the girls to the large parlor on the right where the ceremony will be held. It is filled with rows of these same armless chairs, upholstered in faded satin. Tom and the girls stand on the verge of entering, tentative, waiting for Holly to join them. She watches them for a moment, the backs of their heads together in innocence, and sees that Tom has taken the girls by the hand. It is frightening for them, perhaps he senses, to be here in the presence of death.

The open register rests upon a waist-high stand, its pages expansive, crisp, lined with blue rules where all those who come and only visit sign their names. Holly takes up the golden pen from its holder and looks at her girls standing with Tom, holding his hands, and signs her name, *Mr. and Mrs. Thomas Dunham,* trying it on for size of the building is smaller than he remembered, all of our memories are inflated by the feelings we deposit inside them. It is not the same, standing here in front of the building on the steps of the monument, the precise point where he imagined himself standing when he started sketching it a few days ago. For one thing, a ten-foot-high chain link fence has been erected around the building, to keep people out, and the structure is surrounded by the machines the demolition crew will use to tear it down. A giant crane towers over it, with a battered wrecking ball dangling from a cable. There are other machines here too, bulldozers waiting to pile up the rubble. The building is shabby, worn out, the limestone façade encrusted with car exhaust and pigeon droppings—why not get rid of it, make way for something new?

He had expected to feel a wave of nostalgia standing here, the same torrent of sights and sounds and emotions that made him angry with his wife over the weekend, but seeing the building in its current state has drained all those treacherous visions from his head. Now he is simply tired, his eyelids fuzzy and sore from the truncated night of travel he just endured. Thinking about the past, all those days gone by when he was here with Amelia and Louise, when they were young and still had everything to live for, fills him with a fatigue so heavy that he must sit down on the steps of the monument. He closes his eyes and reaches his arms to the sky; small bones in his neck crackle as he tilts and rotates his head. He yawns luxuriantly, stretches his arms to their fullest extent, and opens his eyes to inspect the old theater and its adjoining hotel one last time. He has always had a ruminating interest in things that have been abandoned, and the current state of this well-loved building interests him from this aspect, the actuality of it compared to the way he has always pictured it in his mind's eye.

The storefronts that lined the first floor on the hotel side are vacant now—the spot on the south corner where the drugstore used to be has empty plate glass windows and a neon HAAG'S sign that will never be lit again. The elaborate marquee that juts above the theater entrance delivers a final message to the small throng of onlookers who have gathered to inspect it: THA NKS FO R THE ME MOR IES, the hand-placed letters unevenly spaced. Tattered curtains linger in the upper-story windows on the hotel end. He had heard that it no longer operated as a hotel, but had been converted in recent years to a nursing home, an unfortunate indication that the building had assumed the same downward spiral of decline as its elderly residents.

In the package sent by the high school alumni committee urging him to attend his class reunion, the invitation mentioned that the theater was seldom used these days, mainly for ceremonial banquets and special occasions. It noted that the last live performance on the main stage was a production of *Hamlet* by the Horace Mann High School Drama Club on October 17, 2004. The last motion picture shown to a paying audience at the theater was *The French Connection,* more than thirty years ago. It was a fabulous place to watch a movie. He can remember sitting towards the front and craning his neck up at the enormous screen from the plush purple seats—filling his entire field of vision with images from the film. But he no longer lives here—

he long ago abandoned this city where he was born. The young people who do live here now probably look at this place as an eyesore, a pocket of blight at the center of their business district. The twin cupolas at either end of the building have turned green with oxidation; otherwise the building appears structurally sound. He can imagine the high cost of upkeep though, the outrageous heating and cooling bills for a half-empty building. Perhaps there is asbestos insulation to deal with. It is time to get rid of it. They will probably build something better here, a flawless new office building that will give people a place to work and reflect the statue of the lady at the top of the monument in its gleaming glass windows.

Everything must come to an end. Sooner or later, every animal, building, and person must make way for another one to take its place. When his plane was landing at the Chicago airport, he saw from the window on the final approach an abandoned road in the middle of the airfield that appeared to lead nowhere, a washed out yellow stripe still visible down the middle, the many cracks in the pavement spawning weeds. He wondered where this road once led, at one time probably a two-lane country highway that traversed a rural landscape of farms and modest houses. A place somebody once called home. Like the theater, the road had outlived its usefulness. Tris wondered how long ago it had been abandoned. And whose job it was to make the decision to scrap it?

More onlookers have gathered on the steps of the monument to gawk, office workers and shop clerks thankful for this diversion from their routine. Tris stands up again and yawns.

Workers with orange hard hats cluster around the base of the crane, motioning to the man who sits in its belly to operate it. Everything must go. That's the thought that enters his head. And now is the time. He flips open his cell phone and sees that he is running late, always running late. The funeral will be starting soon.

He came here with every intention of seeing her one last time. But observing this building has made him understand that this place is no longer part of him. He can never recapture the moments that he lived here. If he went to the funeral, everything he ran away from all those years ago would be dredged up again. Who would be there, Louise and her indigent sons? Why on earth would he want to face them again? Elmer died years ago. And Amelia now is dead and gone. There is no reason to put himself, or her family, through something like that.

One of the workers wearing a white hardhat—perhaps it is the foreman—approaches the fence and shouts for people to stand back. They must retreat across the circular plaza to the sidewalk that surrounds the monument and watch from there. More people have gathered in front of him, so Tris moves up a couple of steps to get a better look. From nowhere, as he turns again to study the building, an image of Amelia as a young woman shoots through his head, like a vision that has been dropped on him from the great height of the crane. Amelia, standing in profile, for an instant pausing to say something, as she walked across the dining room of the old house on Dearborn Street, the side of the double she lived in growing up. There are many people gathered at the table; it is a holiday dinner of some sort—not Christmas or Thanksgiving. In his memory, it has more the raw, damp feel of Easter on an April day when flurries of snow crowd down from the low clouds. Amelia, in profile, had what they called back then "a figure."

She must have been fourteen or fifteen, just entering high school, with hips that narrowed to a waist and modulated out again to her breasts held high by the push-up bras in favor in those days: A figure. Not like the skinny, muscular young women he sees now at the fitness rooms in hotels, running on treadmills and lifting weights so their arms will have sharply defined triceps and their bellies will be flat and hard as a teenage boy's. Amelia stood there, for a moment, one tick of the clock, and her profile moved him to love her. It was at that moment that the chance experimental groping that had taken place once or twice during their childhood adventures was transformed into the realization that he was actually in love with her, beyond the infantile sensations of pure sex, beyond a passing hormonal attraction: He loved her because she was like a calm, deep pool of water, reflecting back to him the absolutely best image of himself he could imagine, the image of himself that he always wanted and expected to see. She could mirror back to him everything he did and everything he wanted to become because her actions were completely un-selfconscious, as gentle and unassuming as the bending frail branches of a tree buffeted by the wind. She never, in his experience, thought to build herself up beyond what she actually was, she never sought to be anything more than this simple and pleasant girl going about her business, enjoying each day—and she did have an appetite for enjoying each day. She loved to eat, and she loved her movies and the garden in the back of the house, and it became clear to him, even as he saw her figure outlined against the breakfront stacked with serving plates and mismatched pieces of crystal and a porcelain vase limned with red peony blossoms, that she loved him too.

In the very next moment, in the instant when his vision of Amelia standing in profile is about to take another step, he hears a creaking sound of rumbling iron machinery and looks up to witness the spinning mass of the wrecking ball slam into the façade of the Lyceum Theater, knocking chunks of limestone from the rows of windows that line the fourth floor, shattering the subtle and intricate rhythm of the structure forever. A thin haze of dust is released as the dislodged chunks of stone fall to the earth. A firehose suspended from the midsection of the crane sends a spray of water towards the gash in the wall, to disperse the plume of dust that has been extracted from the broken stone face of the building. The sparse crowd on the monument steps, some of whom are armed with video recorders and phones that snap pictures, lets out a low murmur of appreciation for the power of dead weight slung along an arc. The crane operator jerks the machine back on its tractor treads, eliciting a high-pitched beeping noise as a warning to whomever may be behind it. Maneuvering the truss of the crane away from the building again sends the wrecking ball back, back, a cruel pendulum that hangs for a moment at the highest point, then, inevitably, returns along the path of destruction, thumping against another section of the wall. The walls are coming down, the structure that held these memories together for so long is broken. Make way! Make way for the new

priest at St. Monica's, I have only been here in this parish for three months now; I was not even here for Easter or the Annunciation. Yet, I must fulfill today one of the most solemn duties that a parish priest can do." Holly can see, even from the fifth row of chairs, where she and Tom and the girls have respectfully taken up their position at the rear of the small gathering of relatives and friends, that the pastor has a thin gloss of sweat in the channel between his upper lip and his nose. His complexion is dark, and the suggestion of a beard is evident, a shadowy crescent from the sideburns across the shallow ridge of his cheekbones. He is young, perhaps in his early thirties.

"And to those many of you who do not know me and have not heard me preach at our church, I apologize in advance if my speaking in the accent of my native land makes it difficult for you to understand my words."

Holly glances towards Tom, another man of words, to see if he has any reaction to this rather aggressive tone, as if the man resents in some way being forced to eulogize the woman lying in the casket behind him. The priest does have a hint of a Mexican accent, but he is clearly quite comfortable composing his sentences in English. Tom stares forward with a hint of a smile on his face, his dark suit jacket and the firm white crease of his shirt collar making him appear trimmer than usual and more handsome, but the smile is likely a result of something he is thinking about from work, a comment someone made at the

Statehouse. He will often relate to Holly offhand quips that he finds hilarious, jokes that he chuckles over which she can neither understand nor laugh about without feeling like a child who has overheard the adults at a cocktail party telling a tawdry story.

"Amelia was a great and kind lady." The priest continues with the awkward formality of someone who has learned the language in a classroom, from a textbook. "I did not know her well. But I have spoken with many of you, friends and family and fellow parishioners alike, and you have given me a pitcure of her kindnesses, her commitment to the church. From her few family members here remaining in the city, I have heard you tell of her great love of children, of her patience with them whenever nieces and nephews paid a visit."

"St. Augustine tells us that patience is the companion of wisdom, and I have always found it to be so. You have seen it in her—this is how she lived. And I have seen it in her too. In my brief but happy times with Amelia at the church, I have seen a woman who was devoted to her faith, and to the Catholic church, who did not abandon the parish of her youth, even though it has seen many changes over the years. This is the sign of a woman with patience, with wisdom. With faith."

The priest brings his hand to his mouth and wipes the sweat from his lip. The silken fabric of his vestments rustles as he moves, lending every motion an extra weight, an added meaning.

"I have seen her working among the many Latino members of our church, which is now a mainly Mexican parish, as if she were among her own family, helping with the difficult work and tedious preparations that the Christmas Benevolence committee is even now undertaking to make sure there is food on the table and gifts in the little children's hands on the magical and most holy day when our Lord and Savior Jesus Christ was born."

He takes a deep breath and darts his eyes around the room, as if he suspects that the small group of people gathered here might have somehow stumbled in to the wrong service. "I did not know her well, but you did know her. You knew her as the sister of that most revered pastor of St. Monica's Church, the Reverend Karl Geist, who founded ministries across the ocean in Japan and China, who is still spoken of in the parish as a famous and—how you say—charismatic preacher from years ago."

In the brief pause as the priest takes a breath, Holly can hear another voice, just above a whisper. "I like the way that lady's hair puffs out of her hat." It is Jenny, trying to amuse herself, and her sister, by making fun of someone, one of the chief pasttimes of a bored teenager. Holly glares at Jenny, purses her lips, and shakes her head in a silent "No."

"I did not know her well, Amelia Geist, but one thing I do know for certain about her is that she is even now still alive and well and sitting this day at the right hand of God with our Lord and Savior Jesus Christ. For the Holy Bible tells us that God, who is rich in mercy, by his great love, even when we were dead in sins, has quickened us together with Christ, and has raised us up together, and made us sit together in heavenly places in Christ Jesus."

Holly can sense that the room has gotten quieter in the face of this bold statement from the priest. "The Holy book tells us, it lets us know that even *you* he has quickened," and he glances from one person to the next among the half-empty rows of armless chairs, "you who were dead in trespasses and sins."

Holly watches the little black-haired preacher with apprehension. He has veered abruptly from a bland and harmless reminiscence into a territory where his statements have the tenor of boastful self-assurance on the one hand and, at the same time, the cryptic ramblings of a fool. She can see that he is clearly nervous in front of his audience, whether it is because of the unfamiliar syntax of his second language or the company of strangers from outside the parish, she cannot be sure. But she knows from experience that anyone who speaks so assertively about a topic is usually trying to cover something up. Either he doesn't believe what he is saying, or he thinks the people he is saying it to won't believe him.

"For by grace are you saved through faith," he continues, "and not of yourselves: It is the gift of God." Holly has always been good at tuning out words like this when someone starts preaching at her. She can tell when someone is trying to tell her that she should be doing something a certain way, for her own good. And this guy is giving off the vibe: Do this, believe what I say, and you can get to heaven, just like the dead woman behind me in the box. Well, Holly knows a few things about that woman too. She has touched her cold body, and it is not going anywhere. She has washed that woman's hair for the very last time.

"These are things you must know, about Amelia, about all of us. This is the gift of God, that He is all around us, He is with us every moment of our lives. He has always loved us, and always will." The priest's dark eyes flit from one face to another, looking for acceptance, trying to make a connection.

"God is never late. He will never abandon us. And the Original Sin that everyone has heard so much about is nothing more than this: It is the belief, the mistaken belief, that we are separate from God."

The priest pauses and emits a ticklish cough, from the back of his throat. He takes a glass of water that is resting on the podium in front of him and drinks from it.

"Original Sin, the trespasses and sins He saves us from, by grace, is nothing more than a belief—a mistaken belief—in two powers: Good and Evil. But I know," he thrusts his hand up at the low ceiling, "I know, and so does every other man of faith, that there is only one power in this universe, and that is God. Deus. Dios. Not two powers, only one."

Holly looks over at Tom, to see if he is reacting to any of this. He still has the faint trace of a smile on his face, as if he has been reliving in his mind a particularly satisfying point of contention with his colleagues and adversaries in the stuffy conference rooms he inhabits. He must feel at home here, Holly thinks, dressed up in his suspenders, among the big words and the painstaking efforts to drive home a point. He and the priest are two of a kind—convincers, salesmen at heart.

"I have always struggled with a way to make this idea seem more real to the people in my parish, who see a world around them filled with many terrible things, raping, killing, children who go to bed hungry at night. The other day I was looking around in the basement of the church, an old building filled with many dusty things from long ago, and I saw a lantern that was probably used to light the building in the days before the electricity came. I picked it up and observed it—for some reason it caught my eye among all the other things there—and I saw that it had a lot of very small holes, cut into the tin to make a pattern with the light that would shine from the lamp. And behind this, another piece of tin that slides across to close it, to shut off the light."

"And the thought came to me: This is how it is when we die. We are each of us points of consciousness—*conocimiento*, we say in Spanish—points of light, that comes from God. And when the tin slides across one of the points of light to close it, when one of us dies, the light it was a part of does not go away—the light that came through that hole is still there and part of the entire light. It is one with it."

Yes, Holly thinks, he is struggling. This idea of a life being like a lantern—she can sense that the others in the room are growing uncomfortable by the shuffling of feet and the adjustment of collars or cuffs. She looks around at the group of people, many of them at least sixty years old, a couple of them younger, hispanic. They came here to see the old lady one last time and hear a few kind words about her; they shouldn't have to stand through this.

"That is why it is the gift of God. We cannot do anything to achieve it." A smile lights up his face, as if he has realized himself for the very first time why he is saying these things. "This is Grace—it is inevitable, it is in the nature of things, when we make out of two things—separateness from God, Good and Evil—one. When we realize that God does this as a matter of course, this is Grace, the realization of God's abiding

love   for

this woman must have been such that he idealized her, he propped her up in his mind as being something she could never be once he left her, a much more attractive version of the woman who actually remained behind here in Middlesborough, living out her life in solitude, padding herself with excess flesh perhaps in an effort to protect herself from any further painful encounters with a man.

The sight that confronts Tris as he stands in a small alcove, an open closet tucked into one side of the main parlor, where coats and jackets might be hung on a much colder day than this, has the power to stop him in his tracks. He is always running late, and so he has become expert over the years at making a stealthy entrance to events such as this, a latecomer to church who knows how to shuffle silently to his seat of dishonor at the back pew during a hymn, a laggard to business meetings and conference calls who knows to remain quiet for a few moments and then blend in to the discussion as if he has always been there.

This time he has sought to slide in through a little-used entrance near the front, where the priest is giving his lecture, mistakenly thinking that it would be closer to one of the rows of chairs and less conspicuous than the large main doorway where the official register stands guarding the room, but now he remains rooted to the spot in this alcove, stunned by the vision of the first girl he ever kissed lying flat on her back in a satiny lavender casket. If he had not known this is who he was coming to see, perhaps he would not even have recognized her. Had she been one of the crowd of people watching the Lyceum meet its doom, he might not have looked twice. Yet here she is, the features of her face distended by years of added fat and distorted by the foreshortened angle from which he stares at her over the open lip of the casket.

The elaborate formality of this room, and the box she is in, somehow makes the astonishment of seeing her this way unbearable. It would be better if they displayed her in a plain pine box. The plush, cushiony sides of the coffin are too much, an effort to gloss over the truth that everyone here can see: Amelia is gone. The girl he knew as a teenager has been gone for years; she was buried long ago, and only the faintest remnants of that person must have lived on with her beyond the day he left her.

If he concentrates, he can make out the features of her face that he once recognized, the compressed, rosebud mouth, the broad forehead, the eyebrows slightly raised, as if she always expected to be asked a question. But the skin is a shade of gray he has only seen in skies that threaten rain, and the cheeks have been rouged in a clownish attempt to hide what everyone can plainly see. The hair still clings to a remnant of the blond he remembers, but it has been flattened and shortened by death and by time. The lips are pursed shut, manipulated by the undertakers into a contour that would not dare to suggest a smile.

Perhaps he had a premonition of her death, through some un-definable connection, and he has been mourning these past few days not her, but the missing part of him that was lost when he made the decision more than fifty years ago not to see her any longer—mourning the unfulfilled potential, the life he might have lived.

But who's to say he would have been any happier had he chosen to stay with her, to remain at home here in Middlesbor-ough? Perhaps he is merely mourning the fact that he must choose, at every step in life, one place over another, one person over another, and these choices only serve to narrow him, to dwindle him down to a single straight line and, finally, to a soli-tary, terminating point. These choices have defined his life by constructing a set of infinite impossibilities, all the many things he will never see or have or do.

He peeks around the corner of the vestibule to examine the remainder of the room. He must remain still here. Someone will notice him, lurking behind this wall. A few people scattered among the rows of chairs—Louise's sons, two of the three it appears, have made it. And there is Louise herself, she did show up, looking for all the world as if she has just floated in from a garden party she might at any moment decide to rejoin, with her head tilted up towards the ceiling beneath a wide-brimmed summer hat. He takes half a step more to get a better look, and he can see

that it is him, the man she spoke to from California. Looks like he made it after all. She had thought he would not come, after speaking to him for a few awkward moments on the

phone. It had seemed either too painful or too much of a has-
sle—she couldn't be sure which—for him to make the long
journey on such short notice. But here he is, standing, for some
reason, among the unused coat hangers in the vestibule. He may
be ashamed of arriving late.

The priest is droning on, but he has lost his audience. Holly
looks around to see whether the others are still listening, but
they do not seem to be affected by his words. They are hearing
what they want to hear. Or they are tuning him out completely.
Most of them would rather be somewhere else; they would
rather not have to think about things such as this. The sooner
he is done with his speech, the sooner they can all go back to
the business of living their lives.

"But now in Christ Jesus, you who sometimes were far off
are brought near by the blood of Christ."

She can see that he is struggling. And she can tell, instinctively, that he must believe, at some level, the things he is saying. How could he not? But he looks from one to the next at
the people shifting their weight and scuffling their feet impa-
tiently among the rows of armless chairs, searching for someone
who will greet his words with a smile of recognition. "For He is
our peace, who has made the two one, and has broken down
the middle wall of partition between us; for to make in Himself
out of two one new man, so making peace."

She wants to meet his eyes and show him that she understands, but these things are better left to the lawyers and the
priests, these fine points of rhetoric and reason.

"Through Jesus we both have access by one Spirit unto the Father." There is something in the way he says this that lacks conviction. He is letting it slip—he knows his words are not enough for something this big. And these words, the droning of his voice, and the trace of a lisp, are making her head throb again. Two tight spots at the back of her neck. The wound on her wrist is knitting together nicely, but she should not be here. They were talking about keeping her in the hospital for a week.

Through the fog of her headache, Holly hears a chair scrape against the wood floor and sees the girls picking at each other again, out of boredom. Zoe is tugging at the hem of Jenny's dress, slyly keeping her hand at her side so no one else will see, because she knows this will annoy Jenny and perhaps force her into an act of retaliation. Holly is close enough to reach over and give Zoe a quick smack on the hand, and is about to, when she sees Tom put his hand on Zoe's shoulder, gently, the way a genuine father would, and calmly whisper to her: "No."

And then, when she is about to smile at Tom, to give him the look she has been thinking about giving him all through the service, a sudden, preening movement deflects into the corner of her vision.

She looks in the direction of that shy man hunched in the vestibule with the suspicion that it must be him, but it is only a fluttering aura in the mirror directly behind him. A bird, caught in flight within the particular angle of the mirror's glass, a trembling image reflected from the window on the opposite side of the room. In a play of the unyielding sunlight, the bird tosses its wings another time and is gone, leaving only the face of that man, and she can see now what she must have also heard in his weary voice over the phone, that he has always

loved this woman lying in the casket, who has lived a separate life, beyond his ability to imagine. The thought of all the days stacked one upon the other in which they both inhabited this earth, separated by thousands of miles and more than that, makes him shudder. All the other women he has known, the two or three others he dated in college, the one he eventually married, were nothing more than pallid replacements for this first woman. He has always been a prisoner of convenience. He settled upon Laura as his wife because she had left him behind after senior year, and it seemed if he didn't follow her and ask her to marry him, he would be making the same mistake twice. He would not lose his nerve again. That's what it had all boiled down to, when he heard what Louise had done that day and how furious Amelia's father had become, he had simply lost his nerve and left Amelia, standing on a corner, alone.

In the space between that memory and the present moment, time collapses, then expands outward, grows immense; a series of concentric circles receding away from the present, ripples in a black pond disturbed by a falling pebble.

There was a foot, a young girl's foot in a sock hanging off the edge of a hammock. The foot bounced, and in bouncing, the ankle tipped the hammock, rolled her body closer to him. The heat of her tucked inside the envelope of the hammock with him; only the two of them and the sky deep and cloudless above, the branches of the pinoak tree swinging side to side as they swung. The sound of the bells ringing, heavy and dense, their iron lambent noise drawing the deep crescent of sky and her body closer together with him, swinging, swaying, all together as one. He understands that he has always loved

me and always will, he has always been with me, a solitary star in the first breaking of the dawn. This thought, this realization, comes to me like a light in the distance, and I know that he will never leave me. Now I know he never did.

I slip away from the hands that bind me. I am lighter than water, lighter than air. I am lighter than darkness and night. Restore to me the bright smooth flame, the dawn of white-hot filaments enormous singing into one another, singing into waves of candles glittering, radiant and white.

Sheer immensity sweats away all sins. I embroider all the wreathed and savoured offerings, in entrance caught by pure delight; I launch the tumbling hasted river. I behold the firmament of halfmoon, the vivid purest ray, gently universal and serene.

When two of you agree, it shall be done. So today I am in union, the marriage of my Soul and my Spirit, through this unison remembrance, sanctified and whole.

About the Author

Chris Katsaropoulos is one of the founders and partners at
Emergent Learning LLC, developers of educational content for
major publishers. He has traveled extensively in Europe and
North America, and enjoys collecting books and music. *Fragile*
is his first novel.